Copyright 2020

Laurence E Dahners

ISBN: 9781674874814

A Pause in Space-Time

A Stasis Story #1

Laurence E Dahners

Other Books and Series

by Laurence E Dahners

Series

The Ell Donsaii series
The Vaz series
The Bonesetter series
The Blindspot series
The Proton Field series
The Hyllis family series

Single books (not in series)

The Transmuter's Daughter
Six Bits
Shy Kids Can Make Friends Too

For the most up to date information
go to
Laury.Dahners.com/stories.html

Author's Note

This novella is the first book of the Stasis Stories

Table of Contents

Chapter One

Kaem Seba's junior year

To Gunnar Schmidt's surprise, the kid took off an old-fashioned wristwatch—not just old-fashioned Gunnar thought, but truly old—and laid it inside the mirrored chamber of the device Gunnar'd assembled. Gunnar studied the kid for a moment, thinking he somehow seemed older than the college junior he claimed to be.

The distractingly pretty Arya Vaii bent down and used her phone to take a picture of the watch sitting in the chamber.

"Wait," the kid said. "Set your phone so the picture displays the time."

"I'm pretty sure I can change the settings and have it display the time later," the girl said, starting to close the door on the chamber.

The kid said, "And if you can't? Why not make sure it's working right? Now. *Before* we send the watch forward?"

The girl rolled her eyes and said, "Come on Kaem. This thing *isn't* going to work the first time we try it." Sotto voce, she followed with "Probably ever." Nonetheless, she started talking to her phone's AI, asking it to display the time on photos.

Send the watch forward? Gunnar wondered. The watch was already sitting at the front of the chamber. *Forward where?* He shook his head. The kid alternated between seeming like a complete ignoramus and knowing bizarrely esoteric stuff. *A brilliant moron. A genius with no common sense. The kind of guy who could build the world's most exotic car but wouldn't know how to drive it.*

While Gunnar'd been mulling the kid's idiosyncratic intelligence, he and the girl had worked out how to have the camera display the date and time the way they wanted it. Then she'd taken another picture. Now it was the girl's turn to say, "Wait, I'm going to video this, so we can show the watch was running when we closed the door."

In a snarky tone, Kaem said, "I thought it wasn't going to work the first time."

She replied, "It isn't, I'm practicing so I'll know how to do the recording right, someday in the future. If it *ever does* work." She snapped the phone onto a mount, positioned the mount, and checked the image the phone was displaying.

"'*Ever* does work?!'" the kid quoted, sounding astonished she could think whatever was supposed to happen to the watch might not.

"*Ever,*" she replied with a roll of her eyes. "The chance this smoke-and-mirrors theory of yours is going to work has to be infinitesimal." She closed the door on the chamber and flipped the latch. Turning back to the kid, she said, "Everything's set."

The kid nodded and pushed the button on one of the units in the pile of electronic equipment he had on the cart. Gunnar heard the whine of capacitors charging. A moment later, there was a snap as they discharged. The girl looked at the kid and then winked at Gunnar. "That's it? No drumroll? No ascending series of notes performed by a hundred voice choir?"

The kid said, "Come on Arya. We've worked so hard for this moment. Don't ruin it with your bitter pessimism."

She shrugged, "Pessimism wards off disappointment when everything goes to hell." She checked the image on her phone. "What do we do now? Check back in... what'd you set it for?"

The kid looked surprised. "No! Open the door and see if the watch went forward."

Gunnar finally spoke, "'Gone forward?' What're you meaning by that?"

Arya answered, holding her hands up and using her fingers to make little air quotes. "Gone forward in time." As she spoke, she used one hand to flip the latch on the door to the small chamber. She continued, "The genius here thinks his theory let you build us a time machine." She tugged at the door but it didn't open.

Astonished, Gunnar said, "Time machine?! You're kidding, right?"

The girl shook her head, tugging harder on the door of the chamber, though it still didn't open.

"Who's funding this?!" Gunnar asked, unable to believe anyone would waste money on a freaking time travel project. *Or waste my time on it! Not that anybody gives a damn about* my *time.*

"I am," she said. "Or maybe Richard Curtis," she continued, naming an immensely wealthy hedge fund founder. "You could say he funded it by giving me a full scholarship with a big enough allowance that I could save money from it." She eyed Gunnar, "This door's really stuck. You have any ideas?"

This finally got Gunnar's attention. He stepped over and tugged on the door's handle himself. The handle felt like it gave a tiny bit but certainly didn't give the sensation it was about to pop loose and come open. He tugged on the top and bottom corners of the door. They gave a little bit as well. "It's as if the radar emitter's caught on something..." he said, mostly speaking to himself.

"What?" Arya asked, though the question seemed rhetorical because she immediately followed up with, "That emitter's in the *middle* of the door. There's nothing in the chamber for it to catch on."

"I know that much!" Gunnar said, irritatedly. "I built the damn thing and saw you put the watch in there. I'm just saying that, when I pull on the door, it feels like the part that's being held, i.e. the part that's keeping the door from coming open, is in the *middle* of the door." He shrugged, "And, that's where the radar emitter is."

"Could it be that running the radar and the laser simultaneously heated the chamber enough that when the air cooled it created a vacuum?" Arya asked.

Gunnar shook his head, "When I pull hard on the corner, I see a little crack open at the top of the door. It isn't big, but it would've broken a vacuum's seal."

"Well, it can't be the microwave emitter," Arya said with certainty. "There's nothing for it to catch on. It must be something else with the door. Was it catching at all before? Maybe the radar or laser caused some part in the hinge or closure to expand a little?"

Frustrated, Gunnar ground out, "The *only* thing that was catching 'before' was the latch. You want me to pull hard enough to break whatever's holding? If whatever's got it caught is something I did wrong, I'll fix it for free. But, if whatever is wrong *isn't* my fault, it's gotta come out of your budget."

The two young people looked at one another. Kaem shrugged, "We've gotta know what's going on in there.

If the watch didn't jump we need to know about that too."

Arya frowned, "But, what if something about the jump froze the door? Maybe all we've got to do is wait for the watch to arrive in the future and we'll be able to open the door? How long did you set it for?"

"Half a kilosecond. But I really don't think our equipment is going to be very accurate on the times."

"So that's about... eight minutes or so?"

Kaem snorted, "About, yeah. Plus or minus about sixty minutes I'd guess. Our components aren't exactly the highest quality, you know?"

"Bitch, bitch, bitch," Arya said. "You'd complain even if your executioner's ax was sharp. Let's at least give it ten minutes before we break the door."

~~~

Twenty minutes had passed. The door still wouldn't open. Resignedly, Arya waved a hand at the little box, "Go ahead, break the damned door."

Gunnar had pulled on the top corner of the door and was forcing a blade screwdriver into the crack that appeared when the kid said, "Oh, crap!"

"What?" Gunnar said, wiggling the screwdriver back out a little way and hoping he hadn't cracked the glass of the mirror on the inner surface of the door. It'd be especially irritating to have broken it moments before Kaem said not to open the door.

Sheepishly, the kid said, "I made a math error. I set it for half a megasecond instead of half a kilosecond."

"And how long's a megasecond?" Gunnar asked.

"11.6 days," Kaem said morosely.

Gunnar leaned up away from the box, pulling the screwdriver out of the crack. "You wanna wait for 5.8 days?"

Laurence E Dahners

"No," they said simultaneously.

Unhappily, Arya said, "go ahead and break the door."

Gunnar sighed, hoping they understood he was upset that they were wasting all the work he'd put into building it. He reinserted the screwdriver in the crack at the top of the door and twisted it. He heard the glass of the mirror crack with several sharp pops. The door sagged open just far enough for him to get his fingers in.

But it still didn't swing freely.

Peering in the small opening, Gunnar saw wire stretched from the center of the door to the opening of the chamber. More interestingly, somehow, the mirror seemed to have come free from the door and was stuck in the opening of the chamber. *Or,* he thought, when he saw that the door itself still appeared to be mirrored, *just* part *of the mirror's stuck in the opening of the chamber.* This was possible, since the mirrored lining of the inside of the chamber consisted of glass silvered on both sides. This trapped the light from the lasers between the two mirrored surfaces of the glass that completely surrounded the chamber. As Gunnar understood it, the differences in EM wave frequency between the laser light trapped in the glass and the radar frequency waves bouncing around inside the chamber was supposed to produce the effect Kaem was hoping for.

Gunnar shook his head disgustedly, *Time travel! Who would've thought I was wasting my time on some idiot's attempt at time travel!*

"What do you see?" Arya asked.

"Part of the mirror's stuck in the opening of the chamber," Gunnar said before he realized that having a mirror on the door *and* in the opening would mean that the glass of the mirror in the door had been split down its middle to provide a mirror in the opening and still leave mirror on the door. "Um…" he said as his mind tried to catch up with what he was seeing.

"Well, it's already completely ruined then," Kaem said. "Go ahead and pull it the rest of the way open so we can see better."

Gunnar did so. It came open with some ripping and popping. One of the first things he registered was that the radar emitter head *was* still stuck in the mirror in the chamber's opening. A couple of bits of wire trailed from it. The wire ripping out of its opening and then breaking probably explained the ripping and popping sensations. The mirror around the radar head—the mirror still stuck in the opening of the chamber—looked perfect.

When his eyes turned to the door he saw cracks in the mirror where the emitter head had broken free from the glass of the mirror. Bits of wire trailed from that opening as well, but other than that and the cracked mirror, the door looked fine. Unconsciously, Gunnar reached up to scratch his head.

It registered on him that a piece of the cracked door mirror was tilted out so he could see it edge-on. He moved his head back and forth to see that bit of mirror from both sides.

It was full thickness glass, silvered on both sides.

His eyes turned to the mirrored surface filling the opening at the chamber. It was perfect. No pieces were missing. If it wasn't for the emitter head and its trailing wires he would've thought… *Oh, hell, I don't know what I would've thought and I sure as hell don't know what I think now.*

Laurence E Dahners

Arya stepped closer and frowned. "It looks like the mirror just pulled off the door and stayed stuck in the opening."

"No," Gunnar said, tapping the door with a finger, "the door's mirror is still mounted in the door. It would seem that Mr. Seba's little invention *makes* mirrors." He glanced back at Kaem, wondering how he was taking this. The kid had his head tilted back and his eyes closed. Gunnar wasn't sure what that meant. *Is he thinking? Having a petit mal seizure? Feeling disappointed? Depressed?* He caught Arya's eye and pointed at the kid, lifting a questioning eyebrow.

Arya glanced at Kaem, shrugged and turned back to the box. She touched the mirror in the opening. "It's warm," she reported.

Gunnar'd been reaching for the torn wiring. He pulled back. "Wait! We've got bare wires. Is the power still on?"

They both turned to look at Seba. He didn't appear to have heard Gunnar's question. "Kaem!" she said sharply.

Opening his eyes wide and blinking, the kid returned his head to vertical looking dazed. "What?" he asked, sounding puzzled.

"Is the power off?" Arya asked. "We've got bare wires dangling here."

"Yes, the power's off."

"It's okay for me to unplug your cart full of electronics then, right?" Gunnar asked pointedly, not willing to trust the imbecilic Einstein on life or death matters.

"Yes," the kid said, starting to tilt his head back again.

"How can I be sure the capacitor's discharged?" Gunnar asked as he reached over and unplugged the cart.

The kid tipped his head back down to give Gunnar a curious look, "How'd you know there was a capacitor?"

"Heard it charge and discharge."

"Well then, you should know it's discharged."

"Well then," Gunnar said exasperatedly, "I'd like to be sure it's *fully* discharged and hasn't been slowly recharging."

"It hasn't," the kid said, but he reached out and pushed a button. "There. If it *had* any charge on it, it's just been discharged."

Grumpily, Gunnar wished he'd been able to hear a little snap when the kid pushed the discharge button— indicating that there had been some charge left and he'd been right to insist. Arya was reaching for the chamber again so he displayed his irritation by picking up a meter and saying, "Wait till I check to be absolutely sure those wires aren't carrying any juice."

Gunnar checked the wires. They were dead.

Arya touched the surface of the mirror in the opening of the chamber. Puzzled sounding, she said, "Still warm. I swear it's just as warm as it was before."

Gunnar walked over to his workbench and got his infrared thermometer off its hooks on the wall. Walking back, he pointed it at the mirror in the chamber. He said, "Seventy-five degrees. Room temperature. Not *very* warm."

Arya was mumbling notes to her phone. To Gunnar, she said, "What's that in Celsius?"

Gunnar flipped a switch on the temp-gun. "Twenty-four Celsius. Doesn't matter what the measurement scale is, it isn't 'warm' in either one."

Laurence E Dahners

Touching it again, Arya said, "Feel it yourself."

Gunnar did. It felt warm. Like touching a person, not a mirror. And slippery as if it were lightly oiled. "I'll be damned."

Kaem, still not lifting his head, said, "Do you have a contact thermometer?"

"No. Are you thinking something's wrong with my temp-gun?" He surreptitiously pointed the gun at his forearm, getting a reading of ninety-two F (33°C). Not the famous 98.6°F body temperature; those kinds of temperature readings were obtained inside body cavities like the mouth or rectum.

Kaem said, "No. Infrared thermometers measure the 'emitted' infrared energy. That energy's partly what's emitted by the object and partly what's *reflected* by the object. When you point an infrared temp gun at a highly reflective surface, like what you're seeing in the chamber, the gun mostly reads photons reflected from the room and not so many photons emitted by the object. Ergo, room temperature."

Gunnar turned to stare at the kid. He still seemed to be in some kind of trance. *Who the hell knows* that *kind of stuff?!* Gunnar wondered.

"Are you saying I'm feeling my own heat reflected back at me?" Arya asked.

"Maybe?" the kid said, still sounding flat.

"But if I took its temperature with a contact thermometer, I'd get room temperature just like Gunnar did with the infrared gun, right?"

"No, then heat could move to the thermometer by direct conduction. If the mirror in the box is actually hot, you should get a higher temp than seventy-five."

Arya said, "Well, I think it's about a hundred degrees. Something close to body temp anyway." She turned back to the box. She tried to stick her fingernails in around the edges, between the mirror and the box. "I can't get a grip."

Gunnar got out his pocketknife. Showing it to Arya, he said, "You want to try this?"

She stepped aside, "Go ahead."

Gunnar unfolded the small, short blade and started working the point in between the mirrored wall of the chamber and the mirror in the opening. Once he had it in a couple of millimeters, he pried back on the blade. It immediately slipped out.

As if the point of the blade got absolutely no grip on the mirror in the opening!

Gunnar felt the tip of his blade to make sure it was sharp. It was. He worked the point in a little deeper. This time when he pried on it, the mirror on the wall of the chamber bowed outward a little though the mirror in the chamber didn't budge. Gunnar quit when he thought either the blade or the mirror on the wall of the chamber was about to break. *What the hell?!* He thought wonderingly.

He felt the surface of the mirror again. *That's* way *slipperier than an oiled surface!* Wondering whether it'd be okay with the kids who were his employers, but far too curious not to do it, Gunnar placed the point of his knife on the mirrored surface with significant pressure and scraped it sideways. It slid across the surface without any detectable resistance. He knew the metal of the blade wasn't hard enough to scratch glass, but when he'd scraped glass with knives before there was at least a dragging sensation. He looked at Arya.

She'd been watching what he was doing. "Did it make a scratch?" she asked curiously.

He shook his head but reached for the loupes he used for fine work. Putting them on, he looked at the surface more carefully. He couldn't seem to get them to focus on the surface. Lifting the loupes, he looked at the surface with the naked eye. He realized he really couldn't see anything but the things that were being reflected by the surface. *There's no dust!* he thought as he realized that dust and smudges were what you usually saw when you looked carefully at the surface of a mirror. *Actually, you see the dust on the surface of the glass, since the reflective layer's on the back side of a normal mirror.* He leaned close and looked at the surface with and without the loupes. *There's no glass in front of this mirror! We're looking right at the reflective surface and it's absolutely perfect. And,* nothing *sticks to it. And I can't scratch it! What the hell?!*

Gunnar got a file. The hardened steel on a file would scratch normal glass.

However, it wouldn't scratch this surface. *I need a diamond,* he thought, getting up and going after one of his carbide-tipped drill bits. Carbide was right up next to diamond on the Mohs hardness scale.

The bit wouldn't scratch the mirrored surface either.

When he walked back to put away the drill bit, he stopped and pinched up some dust from beneath his band saw. Walking back, he rubbed the dust against the mirrored surface. It fell off. *None* of it stuck. He tried a piece of duct tape. It didn't stick. In fact, now he realized the surface didn't even have a fingerprint after all the touching they'd done.

He looked up and found Arya studying him. "What're you thinking?" she asked.

He tapped the surface, "This isn't the kind of mirror we're used to. There's no glass in front of the reflective surface. We're touching the reflective surface and it's harder than carbide... I assume you know only diamond's *supposed* to be harder than carbide. But diamond's transparent and this surface is perfectly reflective. It's frictionless and *nothing* sticks to it, not even dust or fingerprints." He shrugged, "I don't know what the hell this is, but I'd swear it's the first piece of it that's ever existed on this earth."

"How thick is it?" Arya asked.

Gunnar slid his knife in between the mirror and the wall of the chamber again, then bent a hook into the end of a piece of fine wire. Reaching in with the hook, he couldn't feel anything because the surface was so slippery.

He didn't meet any resistance until the wire was almost deep enough to hit the back of the chamber. Then he felt some resistance to pushing it in deeper. The resistance he suspected came from the narrowing of the space between the mirror and the glass mirror of the chamber's wall, not from friction with the mirror filling the center of the chamber.

There wasn't any resistance to pulling it out either, suggesting that the wire hook hadn't gotten in deep enough to catch on the back corner. He said, "I think it, whatever 'it' is, completely fills the chamber. I'll bet we can't pull it out because it's caught on the radar emitters and other irregularities in the walls of the chamber."

"What the hell? Fills the chamber?"

Kaem suddenly got up and came over. Gunnar drew back and watched as the kid felt the strange surface. He frowned, "I was wrong about how something would get to the future when it was encompassed in the differential fields. It doesn't disappear from now, then reappear at some point in the future. Instead, we're simply stopping time inside the incorporated volume. Presumably, at some point in the future that small section of space-time will start progressing forward in time again."

Arya said, "What?! Then where's your watch? If what you're saying is right, we should be looking at a stopped watch."

Kaem gave her a steady look, "We didn't just stop time for the *watch*. We stopped it for the entire volume of space inside the chamber."

Arya looked back at the device, "And the surface of that volume of space is covered with a mirror?"

Kaem shrugged, "Probably not just the surface. Because time's stopped in there, nothing can get in or out. Everything just bounces off. Fingerprint oils, dust, knife blades, light... It's a mirror for *everything*, not just for light like the mirrors we're used to."

"It's a stasis field," Gunnar said.

"A what?" Arya asked, looking disappointed. Gunnar supposed she thought he'd just said it was something common, not exotic.

"A stasis field. They're a trope in science fiction. A stasis field is a place where time's stopped. Just like what we've got here. In SF they're usually spherical, but they're described as having mirrored surfaces and being impossibly hard."

"So, *not* something real," Arya said disparagingly.

"No," Gunnar said pointing at it, "but anybody who reads science fiction's going to recognize that thing." He gave them a questioning look, "You want me to take that chamber apart so we can really examine it?"

"Can you get it apart without breaking any more of it?" Kaem asked.

Gunnar glanced at it, then shrugged. "Probably going to break the other radar emitters."

"Let's just wait," Kaem said. "In another five, plus or minus twenty days, the stasis should break down and we'll have all our parts back undamaged. Except the front mirror and emitter, of course." He sighed, "Besides, I need time to think this over."

Gunnar really wanted to play with the stasis field.

But it wasn't his call.

Chapter Two

The start of Kaem Seba's freshman Year

A few days before Kaem Seba left home his father suddenly said, "The next few months are gonna be hard for you, aren't they?"

Kaem had nodded uncertainly.

His father shifted uncomfortably, "I'm not sure how to give you advice. All your teachers tell me you're a genius. I realize you learn faster and you surely *know* more than… anyone I've ever been around. However, I think there's a difference between knowledge and wisdom, eh?"

Kaem nodded again, wondering where this was going.

"Now, I haven't been to college. But I left Tanzania and went to Italy. Then I left Italy and came to America. And I can tell you that even a trip to another town… There're new people, and new places, and different ways of doing things. You don't know where to find anything. It's frightening. So, here's my bit of wisdom. *Act* calm. Not only will others think you know what you're doing when you *act* calm, but you'll also start to *feel* calm. When you're sad, make yourself smile and your sadness will be less. When you're frightened, pretend you're brave and the fear will be less provoking."

Kaem had thought this advice ridiculous, but when he'd gotten on the bus for the first solo trip of his life he'd *pretended* it didn't bother him.

And it hadn't!

Afterward, he'd told himself that of course, it hadn't. He knew the numbers. Traveling by bus was safer than riding in a car.

When he'd felt sad that he'd left his family, he'd forced himself to smile. The lady he was sitting next to on the bus had asked him what he was so cheerful about. Kaem didn't tell her his father's theory. Instead, he said, "Somehow I got a scholarship to study at the University of Virginia."

She drew back, "Somehow? You must have done well in school, then applied for it, *that's* how!"

"Um, no. My family was too poor to send me to college so I didn't apply for admission. But a friend of my mother's gave her an old computer and Mom let me use it as much as I wanted after I got home from work. I've been studying online, taking courses through the Khan Academy," he shrugged, "mostly because I like knowing how things work. Then I got a call from a man in Virginia named Richard Curtis. He gives scholarships to kids all around the world."

"Still," she said, "you had to apply for his scholarship, right? So, you *must* have thought it was possible."

"No. Apparently he selects his scholarship recipients based on data provided by Khan Academy. He looks for young people who've passed the higher levels of the Academy's courses." Kaem snorted, "I wasn't even aware it was possible. I was lucky enough to be selected without knowing it could happen. Mr. Curtis even paid for me to take the SAT. When I got into UVA, he sent me a new computer. And, then just an hour before I left, a new phone arrived. It's supposed to be linked to a high-end AI." Kaem shook his head, "Some people say bad things about him. I'm sure Curtis isn't a saint, but he's my hero."

They'd talked on as the bus droned through the night and the pleasant conversation had eased his fears.

When the bus got to Charlottesville, he asked his phone's AI how to get to his new dorm. It was much more capable than the AI on the old low-end phone he'd shared with his sister Bana. He didn't even have much experience with the old dinosaur because she'd carried their phone most of the time. Social media was so important to her that she'd considered it a major imposition when he asked to use the phone.

This new phone immediately told him of a number of ways he could get to the dorm. It turned out that it was only two miles, so he slung the strap of his dad's old army duffel over his shoulder and started walking, following directions provided by his new AI through his earbud. While he walked, he started exploring the capabilities of the phone's AI. He began to appreciate more and more what it'd meant when Mr. Curtis sent the phone. It wasn't just so he'd have a functioning phone, but so that he'd have a truly capable AI. *Which is gonna help me learn,* he thought.

When the phone rang, he wasn't sure what was happening because the sound it made was different from the ring Bana'd installed on their old shared phone. It took him another moment to figure out how to answer it. "Hello?"

"Kaem?"

"Uh-huh."

"Why didn't you call me? My AI says you're already in Charlottesville."

"Um... Who are you?"

"Arya Vaii! Didn't your phone display my name?"

"No, I mean, 'Who's Arya Vaii?'"

"I'm one of Mr. Curtis's scholarship students here at the University. I'm supposed to orient you. I sent you a text telling you to call when you were about to get here. What happened?"

Feeling embarrassed, Kaem said, "I, uh, barely got the phone before I left home. I don't really know how to use it very well yet."

Vaii sighed as if dismayed to be saddled with such a cretin. "Where are you now?"

"Walking to my dorm."

"You've already gotten checked in?!"

"Um, no, I just got off the bus."

"You came on the bus?!" she asked, disbelievingly.

~~~

Kaem's phone rang again as he and several other incoming students walked up to the front of his new dorm. *Holy crap this Vaii girl's impatient,* he thought. He'd promised to call Arya as soon as he arrived at the dorm, but she didn't seem to trust him to follow through. Calling the phone's AI by the name he'd assigned it, he said, "Odin, answer the call."

It wasn't Vaii. Instead, he heard his sister Bana's voice in his earbud. "You got a new phone?!" she asked accusingly. She sounded like she thought he'd committed some grievous wrong.

"Yeah," Kaem said, worried about what he thought was coming. "The scholarship guy, Richard Curtis, sent it to me. It's supposed to help me wi—"

Bana interrupted, "*You* don't care about phones! *Trade* with me! It doesn't matter to you if you have a new phone, but," her voice began to whine, "it'd mean the *world* to me!"

"I think I'm supposed to use it to help with my school—"

"You don't need social media for college," she said dismissively. "Our old phone's plenty good enough for calling home."

"No, it's got a high-end AI that can help—"

"An AI?! Oh! That'd be perfect. Please Kaemy!"

I don't want to argue, he thought, also disgruntled by the use of her pet name for him. "Let me make sure I don't need it for my classes. If I don't, maybe we could swap when I come home for Thanksgiving."

"Can't you mail—?!" Bana started.

Kaem used one of her own tactics, interrupting to say, "Oops, sorry Bana. Gotta go... Odin, phone off." He heard an abbreviated wail from his sister as the connection broke off.

Kaem set down his duffel and looked around the dorm lobby. It was crowded with milling people. Almost all looking younger than he was. There was a line of people waiting to talk to a person behind a desk. Not sure whether he needed to see that person or not, Kaem got in the line, then said, "Odin, call Arya Vaii." He thought. *I hope she intended me to call before I got checked in.*

~~~

Kaem had been standing in line for quite a while. He'd been working with his phone's AI trying to figure out what he was supposed to be doing on arrival here in the dorm. A pretty girl stepped up beside him. He thought she might be Indian, but he hadn't met many people of Indian descent so he wasn't sure. To his surprise, she spoke with Arya's voice, "Looks like I timed it about right, you're almost up to the front."

"Arya Vaii?" Kaem asked.

She nodded.

"How did you know who I was?"

"Asked my phone," she said distractedly. "It brought up a picture." She glanced around, "The people behind you are pissed because they think I'm trying to cut the line. I'm just going to stand over to the side." She stepped away.

As she moved away, a couple of big guys strode up and stepped into the spot she'd vacated in front of Kaem. One turned to him and said, "Thanks for holding our place."

Halfheartedly, Kaem began to protest, "Hey..."

The guy turned back to Kaem. Looking him straight in the eye, he said menacingly, "Hey what?!"

Suddenly, Arya was there. She stepped up so she was right in the big guy's face. Loudly she said, "'Hey,' he was saying, 'I'm *not* holding places for you two snails. Go back to the end of the line where you belong."

The guy blinked, obviously having no idea how to handle her. "Snails?"

"Ugly things. Leave a trail of slime behind them wherever they go... Just like you two."

Somebody behind Kaem giggled. The big man's face reddened. He turned and gave Kaem a high-intensity glare, "You *were* holding us a place, right? Tell her."

Kaem didn't like confrontation and he really didn't think he should make an enemy of a guy this size. He was about to just agree with the guy before he got hurt, but then, out of the corner of his eye, he saw Arya give a sharp shake of her head. When his eyes strayed to her, she was giving him a ferocious look. He turned and looked the big guy in the eye, "You must have me mixed up with someone else. *I* wasn't the one holding your place."

The guy grabbed the front of Kaem's shirt, pulling him close and growling, "You *were* holding us a place, right?"

The word, "sure," was forming in Kaem's mind when, to his utter astonishment, Arya grabbed the big guy by the upper arm, pulled up close, and snarled, "Let go of him before I *hurt* you."

"Get off!" the big guy said, trying to shake her loose. Even while he was doing this, he turned his attention back to Kaem and drew back a fist, "Am I gonna have to…"

Using her grip on the man's arm, Arya practically launched herself up his body to slam her elbow into his nose.

The guy let go of Kaem's shirt, staggering back. Hands clapped to his face, he stumbled into his buddy. The friend made no effort to catch him so he toppled to the side and sprawled to the floor, landing on his buttocks and hands.

Arya was immediately up in the face of his oversized buddy. "Take him to the back of the line, where you two belong!" she bellowed in a commanding voice, pointing back along the line.

This guy put up his hands, "Okay, okay. Let me just check on my friend first."

Arya looked at the guy on the floor, "He's got friends?" She shook her head then turned her eyes back up to the one who was still standing. "Go ahead. But if you count yourself among his friends, you have my pity."

The guy squatted down and said, "You okay?"

His buddy said, "Fine!" then rolled over and started getting up off the floor. Looking angry but sheepish, he started for the back of the line trailing his friend.

Arya turned cheerfully to Kaem, "You okay?"

"Holy crap! Where'd you learn to do that?"

She shrugged, "Got picked on when I was a kid. My mom sent me to karate classes."

Then Kaem was checking in. They took his fingerprints and a DNA swab, then sent a room key to his phone.

Arya walked him up to his room. To his surprise, she helped unpack his duffel bag and put stuff away, all the while keeping up a running commentary about the university. He felt embarrassed having her handle his stuff, but she taught him a surprising amount as they went along. Where to do laundry, find quiet places to study.

How to do this, how to do that.

He found himself sprawled on his own bed. She'd perched on the bed that would belong to his roommate. She filled him in on the social milieu at the university. Suddenly, in what felt to Kaem like a completely unrelated topic, she asked, "What're you going to study?"

"Um," he said, drawing a blank on his classes. The one he remembered was only because he dreaded it. "I've got English…" he trailed off as he tried to remember his other classes, none of which he was enthusiastic about.

"Not what classes you've got, what you want to learn overall. Your major."

"Oh. Time."

"Time?"

He nodded.

"Time's not a major!"

"Oh... I don't really understand majors and minors so I didn't declare one yet. I'm wanting to learn about time. Do you know what major that'd be?"

"Time? You mean... Time management? Saving time? Or..." she looked puzzled.

"Um, no. I mean, stopping time or speeding it up, maybe reversing it."

Arya blinked at him a couple of times. "I think that's physics. But, I'm pretty sure nobody can change the flow of time."

Kaem shrugged, "I think it's possible. I've been working on my own theory."

"Your own theory?! What makes you think you can come up with your own theory?"

"I've read and studied everything I can find on the Internet. Also, on Khan Academy, Wikipedia, Google. Wolfram Alpha. Physics.org"

Her eyes narrowed slightly. "I don't think you can just assemble random crap off the Internet and come up with a viable theory."

Kaem didn't know how to respond to that, so, instead, he asked, "What're you majoring in?"

"Business," she gave him a sly grin. "It's in my blood."

"In your blood?"

"Um, yeah. My family's *always* been in some kind of business. Way back into India, hundreds of years ago."

"Ah," Kaem said as if he understood, though he really didn't. He was glad his curiosity about her heritage had been satisfied without his having to ask though. "And... you want to be a businesswoman?"

"I'm *going* to be a businesswoman." She arched an eyebrow, "A *hell* of a businesswoman. I'm gonna be so rich my assistants won't even let a physics major like you *talk* to me."

"All you need's a little self-confidence," Kaem said, grinning.

"Yeah, yeah. You're going to major in physics, then pound your head on the wall, trying to come up with crazy theories about time. This won't accomplish anything except to maybe get you on the podium of some conference so you and other nerds can pat each other on the back. You'll eventually wind up teaching physics at some university. Pounding numbers into the heads of poor young boys like yourself. Naive idiots who *think* they're going to discover something important but never will."

"Wow, *you're* a pessimistic bummer."

She gave him a dismissive wave, "Optimism's for those who want to have their hearts broken on a regular basis. Pessimism's for realists. When things actually go well, pessimists are over-the-top happy." She stood up. "I've gotta eat. If you're hungry I can show you a good place for a burger."

Kaem stood as well. "I'm hungry, but dirt poor. Is the place expensive?"

"It's on the food plan," she replied.

"Food plan?"

"Didn't you read anything in your scholarship packet?"

"Yeah, but I didn't really understand a lot of it. No one in my family's ever been to college," he shrugged, "so, there hasn't been anyone to tell me how things work. I... I really appreciate your help."

"Don't worry about it. An older student helped me when I started here. It's part of Curtis's requirements. You'll be expected to help a new student next year. So, your scholarship includes a meal plan. You can eat free at certain places. Come on, I'll explain things as we walk."

~~~

Sitting in Bilko's Burgers, Arya studied her new protégé. He had medium-dark skin, curly hair and looked... sick. She'd had to slow her pace on the walk to Bilko's. He seemed older than a college freshman should be. Never afraid to ask questions, Arya said, "Tell me about your family. Where do they live, what do they do, where'd they come from?"

"Um..." he said, looking as if uncomfortable to be quizzed on personal topics. "I'm from a small town in West Virginia. One so small I'm sure you've never heard of it."

He seemed about to go on, so she interrupted, "Maybe I've never heard of it, but as soon as you tell me its name, I will have."

"Valen," he said, then grimaced as if ashamed. "Famous for its meth... And not for much else."

"You're right, I've never heard of Valen," she said, wondering whether he looked sick because he was a meth addict. But, it'd be extremely surprising if he'd made the kind of grades and test scores needed to get a Curtis scholarship while he was hooked on meth. "What about your family?"

"My mom and dad moved here from Italy, hoping to find better jobs and less discrimination."

"And?"

"Their dreams haven't been realized."

"So what do they do?"

"My mom runs a few laundromats and my dad does... odd jobs."

She studied him, wondering how to ask her next question, then decided to just bull ahead. "You look older than most college freshmen."

He shrugged, "Yeah."

"Yeah, you *look* older? Or yeah, you *are* older?"

"Yeah, I'm older. I didn't think I could afford to go to college so I didn't apply. But I did start taking courses through the Khan Academy," he shrugged, "because I like math and really like understanding the way things work. After I'd finished a bunch of their courses Mr. Curtis called me and offered me a scholarship."

"Didn't think you could go to college because your grades were bad?"

"They were okay, 'cause, you know, high school's easy. But we didn't have any money and I didn't do any of the extracurriculars you need to get an all-expenses scholarship."

"Not even any sports?"

He shook his head.

"You look... like you're not in such good health. Is that why you didn't play sports?"

"You're getting' pretty personal."

"You don't have to answer, but if I understand what's going on, maybe I can give you better advice."

He shrugged, "I've got sickle-thalassemia."

Arya blinked, "What the hell's that?"

"I got a gene for sickle cell anemia from my African dad and a gene for beta-thalassemia from my Italian mom. Both diseases make you anemic and sickle cell gives you crises to boot."

"I thought they had gene therapy for sickle cell?"

Kaem shrugged again, "They do. One's approved and there's a couple of trials for new ones. I applied to be in one because we're so poor we could never afford to pay for gene treatment. But, they're only trialing it in people with pure sickle cell right now. Thalassemia has some trials too, but again, only trialing in people with pure thalassemia so far."

"Oh… That's shitty."

He rolled his eyes. "Tell me."

"So, this sickle-thalassemia. It keeps you from playing sports because…"

"I'm so anemic that I don't have the energy to do much. It's bad enough I have to get transfusions every so often. Even better, if I do exert myself and use up enough oxygen, then my red blood cells start to sickle. The sickled cells plug off blood vessels and give me a 'sickle crisis,' where some part of me's cut off from its blood supply and starts dying for lack of oxygen. That hurts like hell. Even better, if one of them happens in my brain someday, it'll be like a stroke. I could find out what stupid's like." He took a deep breath and blew it out, "So I live slow and easy. I just appease big guys; I don't try to punch them out." He gave her an arched eyebrow look, "Thanks again for defending my honor."

She gave him a grin. "No problem. Any time."

"I'll just put you on speed dial for when those oversized assholes decide to take their revenge."

"Oh," Arya said, feeling chagrined. "I didn't think about that."

He gave her a grin that seemed a little forced, "Don't worry about it. If you can't get there in time to save me, I'll just apologize abjectly. If they beat on me anyway, I'll just curl up in a little ball and hope they get tired of bruising their toes."

"Well," she said, doing her best to sound brightly cheerful, "once you invent your time machine, I'll build a business around it. We'll get rich enough you can afford to buy your gene therapy, hire bodyguards and start taking karate yourself."

He lifted an eyebrow, "But *you* don't think there's the faintest chance I can affect the flow of time, do you?"

"You'd better prove me wrong!"

Chapter Three

Kaem Seba's sophomore year

Kaem climbed the stairs to Curtis's mansion, breathing hard with the exertion. *I hope my anemia's not worse already,* he thought, trying to remember how long it'd been since his last transfusion. *Thank Obama for the fact that I could get insurance with my preexisting condition. Thank Curtis that my scholarship included insurance. Thank Medicaid for keeping me alive until I got here.*

It was the annual function for the recipients of Curtis's scholarship, and Kaem was feeling underdressed again. He had on a black turtleneck and black slacks he'd bought at a thrift shop. They were in pretty good condition and he thought he looked okay, but everyone else had on a suit.

Just like last year.

This year Kaem had hoped to find a suit at the thrift shop, but no such luck. *Curtis is going to think I'm such a wastrel. Unable to save enough money out of his generous allowance to buy a suit like everyone else has.*

After all, none of the recipients of Curtis's scholarships were wealthy, but the scholarship provided a fairly generous living allowance. You *should* be able to save some money out of it, and Kaem did, but with his dad finding little work, his family was having a difficult time getting by on what his mother made at the laundromat. Bana called Kaem all the time, telling him how bad things were and urging him to send everything he could. Usually, she also made another plea that they swap phones. She found it impossible to believe Kaem actually used the phone for his studies.

So, he sent every penny he could spare to his mother's account. And he couldn't even afford a secondhand suit. Well, he could've, if there'd been one that fit. They were all too big. What he couldn't afford was a secondhand suit *and* the cost of extensive alterations.

Therefore, a not too tired black turtleneck and slacks.

Kaem looked around for someone he knew besides Mr. Curtis. Curtis made him nervous since the man held the keys to Kaem's life. Kaem had been disappointed to find he didn't like his hero, though he tried to hide his distaste from the man himself. Kaem found Curtis... smarmy. The guy never missed an opportunity to talk about how smart he was, mention his self-made wealth, point out the features of his mansion or the beauty of his young second wife.

The fact that he gave scholarships to deserving poor kids was massively redeeming, and Kaem respected him.

He just didn't like him.

Kaem saw Arya Vaii and started drifting her way. He'd developed quite a crush on her since she'd welcomed him to the university. She was pretty and smart and she'd beat up that big guy who was pushing him around. Those were big selling points. He seemed unable to socialize with her though. He kept finding himself teasing her or otherwise giving her grief.

She was probably a year or two younger than he was, but she was a year ahead of him in school, much better looking, much healthier and more physically fit, really smart... *It's just crazy to keep pining after her,* he thought, *there's no way she's ever going to go for someone like me. Besides, her parents immigrated from India and they're probably planning to arrange her marriage. A marriage to someone of the same or better class.* Not *to a mixed-race mongrel whose parents are broke and doesn't even own a suit.* He stopped drifting that direction and stopped to study one of Curtis's paintings.

Not that he really saw much of the painting, it was just a safe direction to point his eyes.

Arya's voice came over his shoulder, "Hey, I thought you were coming over to talk to me?"

Kaem turned and forced a smile. "I was considering it, but then I realized a high and mighty junior like yourself wouldn't have time for a measly sophomore like me." *She even smells good! Why can't I just say something nice? I could've told her I liked her dress.*

She nudged him with an elbow, "I happen to like measly sophomores, though I'm not sure about you. It's good to see you made it out of your freshman year, I had serious doubts. How're your classes this year?"

"They're okay," he said thoughtfully, "though not as helpful as I'd hoped."

"Helpful? With what?"

"With my..." he suddenly realized she probably didn't remember much about their talks back during his freshman year, "my theory," he finished weakly.

"Oh yeah," she said, as if surprised to remember, "you have a theory about time, right? Did you decide to major in physics?"

He nodded, not sure whether he felt hurt that she didn't remember more, or ecstatic that she remembered him at all. "But the classes I've taken so far haven't delved much into time."

"So, you're doing okay?" She made a face, "Physics is supposed to be *hard*."

"I guess it is for a lot of people," he said. "Quite a few kids have dropped out." He shrugged, "But I like it, so I'm happy to study hard."

She raised an eyebrow, "Even the parts that don't have anything to do with," she lowered her voice to make it sound ominous, "time?"

Kaem grinned and leaned closer, as if divulging a secret, "Even those." He leaned back and, remembering what his mother had taught him about social skills, asked, "How're your business classes coming?"

"They're fine," she said dismissively. "The exciting thing is that I started my own little business."

"Awesome!" Kaem said. Not just because he knew it was polite, but because he really felt happy for her. "What kind of business is it?"

"I came across a little book about local haunted houses. So, I worked up a little walking tour that visits some of them. Then I worked up a bigger tour to visit even more houses in a rental van. I dress up in an old-style costume and tell the stories. It's been busy enough I've hired some other students to guide some of the tours."

"Really? Do you believe in ghosts?"

"No!" She rubbed her fingers together, "I believe in money."

"It's hard for me to believe this town has that many tourists."

"Ah. You're forgetting how many parents come to town to visit their kid's college. They want *something* to do while they're here, so they'd be happy to take a tour even if it wasn't any good." She arched an eyebrow, "And *my* tour is *excellent*." She shrugged, "They pretty much only come when school's in session, which just so happens to coincide with when I can hire students to guide them."

"Ms. Moneybags!" Kaem said admiringly.

"Ms. Moneybags?" Kaem heard Curtis say from behind him.

"Um, yes," Kaem said turning to face the man. "Ms. Vaii was just telling me how she's started a small business on the side."

"Very good!" Curtis exclaimed. Then he launched into the story of the student business he'd launched and how it made a million dollars his senior year. When he'd finished massaging his self-esteem, he turned to Kaem, "A little birdie tells me you're pulling down excellent grades in physics?"

"Um, I'm doing okay..."

Curtis turned to Arya, "'Okay,' in this case means he's getting absolutely the highest scores on *every* test in *every* class."

Horribly embarrassed, Kaem flicked a glance at Arya hoping she wouldn't be too put off. "Not really..."

Curtis said, "Not that it's any great surprise after the way he broke the charts on Khan Academy courses and on the SAT. I mean, I got *great* scores, but Mr. Seba's done even better." He slapped Kaem on the back. "Good work. When you're done you'll have a job with my company even though we don't do physics." He laughed, "Though I'm sure you'll have plenty of job offers that *will* use your skills." He turned and walked away.

Kaem ventured another glance at Arya who was staring at him wide-eyed. He mumbled, "It's not really like he says…"

"It's not? What *did* you score on the SAT?"

"I just had a good day."

"Really? How good?"

"1600," he said softly. Seeing Arya's eyes widen further, he hastened to say, "It's nothing, really. I'm just good at tests. Besides, I'm *not* very good at reading and writing. I don't have any idea how I got an 800 on that section. Must have been really lucky that day."

"Well," she said, consideringly, "I just wish I was that good at business." She stared at him for a moment, then said, "If you're that smart, I definitely want a piece of the action on your theory. When you're ready to build your time machine, let me know and I'll help finance it with the money from my business. Then we'll get you your gene therapy, right?"

She turned and walked gracefully away, leaving Kaem floundered. *She remembered!* he thought. Suddenly, he hurried after her, "Wait. I do have a design already, but not nearly enough money to build a working model…"

She studied him for a moment, "And you think I should invest the profits of my business?"

"Well… you'd have to be crazy I guess."

Her laugh was beautiful. She waved at some chairs. "Let's sit over here so you can tell me about it."

Laurence E Dahners

Chapter Four

In Kaem Seba's junior year again

It was cool and rainy that morning. Gunnar had to start the heater when he went out to work in his shop. He'd been out there about five minutes when he heard a faint "poof" sound behind him. Puzzled, he turned around. It took a few seconds before he realized that the mirrored object filling the chamber in Kaem Seba's little box had disappeared. The watch was lying in the chamber as if it'd never been buried in a stasis field.

As he got out his phone to take a picture, Gunnar thought. *As crappy as the weather is, the barometric pressure's probably pretty low. It was a nice sunny day when Kaem put the watch in stasis. I'll bet the pressure was a bit higher.* He had his AI check the barometer for both days and found a significant difference. *The "poof" I heard was the higher-pressure air in the stasis field suddenly decompressing into the lower atmospheric pressure today,* he thought.

The watch was reading 3:17 p.m. and its date was nine days ago. Gunnar wasn't sure exactly what time they started the stasis field, but it'd been midafternoon and right now it was morning.

Seba's damned field really did stop time, he thought in amazement.

Gunnar sent a text message to Kaem and Arya, attaching the picture he'd just taken. Then he started examining the components in the chamber, especially the radar emitters that protruded into the chamber. As best he could tell they were all fine. Kaem had taken all the external electronic components back with him when he'd left, so there was no way for Gunnar to check whether the emitters were working, even if he'd understood Kaem's setup. The electronics held the real secret of how he induced stasis, so Gunnar could see why Kaem didn't want anybody else fooling around with them.

Because of their classes, it was a couple of hours before Kaem and Arya Uber'd over to look at the chamber and retrieve Kaem's watch. As Gunnar'd told them when they called, there wasn't much to see. The chamber's door was still broken. The rest of the chamber was absolutely fine. "So, it worked," Gunnar said. "What's your next step? Fix the door and try to send a mouse into the future?"

Kaem looked contemplative. He said, "I think we need to build a chamber that doesn't have any bumps on its interior walls. I've got some ideas on how we could use the inner mirrored surface as the radar emitting antenna. That way we'll be able to build a smooth chamber. After all, we need to be able to take the stazed segment of space-time out of the chamber. Then we'd be able to staze other things while we're waiting for stasis to break on the first object."

Arya said, "So we could staze a mouse, and a clock—"

"And a burning candle," Kaem interrupted, waving dismissively, as if those things weren't important. "More interesting, we could just staze some air and run tests on the properties of the stazed segment of space-time."

Arya frowned, "What kind of tests?"

Gunnar said eagerly, "I hope we'd be testing it to see if its surface's really frictionless."

Kaem nodded. "And, how hard is it? Wha—"

Gunnar interrupted, "It's harder than diamond. I bought a diamond glass cutter and it couldn't scratch it."

Kaem nodded again, then continued, "What're its other mechanical properties?" He got a distant look in his eyes, "Now that I've worked with the math, taking consideration of our first result, my theory suggests that the mechanical properties of a segment of stazed space-time may be pretty surprising."

Arya gave him a suspicious look, "What kind of surprising?"

"Essentially we should have an unchanging piece of space-time. If we can't change it, then it'll appear to have zero friction. Hardness *far* beyond diamond. Strength much higher than steel." Kaem shrugged, "The kind of numbers the theory predicts are... kind of impossible to believe. But, still, even if they aren't what my math predicts, they should still be pretty far out there."

Arya gave the broken chamber a worried look. "I don't know. Repairing the chamber we've got sounds doable. Building an entirely new one..." She looked at Kaem, "You don't have any money, right?"

He shook his head, "I save everything I can from my living allowance, but I send it all to my family. They've been having a really tough time."

Arya bit her lip, "I've spent almost all of what I've saved building this one. I think we've got to fix the chamber we've got and do whatever experiments we can with it. That's probably all I can pay for until time passes and my business brings in some more cash." She tilted her head curiously, "If we could work out a viable product, maybe we could sell it and use the income from the sales to finance more experiments." She shook her head and snorted a little laugh. "I really didn't think this would work, so I never considered the next steps. I must've been crazy to invest almost everything I've got in something I didn't think had a chance." She turned to Gunnar with a resigned look on her face. "How much just to repair the door?"

Gunnar said, "Kaem's right. That'd be a waste. The money's going to be in stazed objects that you can take out of the chamber—"

Arya started to interrupt, "We *don't* have the money for—"

"I'll finance it," Gunnar said, "for one percent of your profits."

Arya gave him a wide-eyed look. "You... can afford...?"

Gunnar snorted. "Yeah. I look poor because I *save* my money. I can afford to finance a *lot* of experiments."

***

Kaem had just finished opening the boxes when his roommate got back. "What the hell's all this?" Ron asked.

Remembering his dad's advice, Kaem smiled at Ron, trying to defuse Ron's tendency to belligerence. He waved at the stack of electronic gear he'd ordered on Gunnar's credit, then said, "Just some electronics for an experiment we're doing." Kaem didn't specify who "we" was, hoping Ron would think it was a physics class project. "As soon as I make sure I've got the right stuff I'll take all those boxes down to be recycled."

"Yeah, do that," Ron said in a clipped fashion.

Kaem cleared Ron's side of the room, throwing the boxes on his bed. Then he went over his list of equipment, comparing it to the stuff he'd just unpacked. Not only making sure that he'd got what he ordered, but also looking at the modules to make sure they had the inputs and outputs he'd expected from studying them online.

The new equipment was much better than the setup he'd kludged together for their first trial. For that, he'd bought a few cheap items. He'd had to check out some of the things he couldn't afford from the physics equipment room, but he'd had to return those the next day. Also, the ones available from the equipment room tended to be old and not of the best quality to begin with.

It took him the entire evening, but he finally got set up and, with his new digital oscilloscope, was able to show the equipment producing all the frequencies he wanted with much greater precision than his previous gear.

As a bonus, the new set up was much smaller. It'd be a lot easier to haul around.

Kaem took the boxes down to recycling. He checked the time. Deciding Gunnar wouldn't be in bed yet, he spoke to his AI, "Odin, call Gunnar Schmidt."

"What do you want?"

Not sure whether this was Gunnar's usual grumpiness or something worse, Kaem said, "Um, I was wondering how you're coming on the new chambers?"

"Why? Did you finally get the electronic gear?"

"Uh-huh. It looks really good. I'm dying to try it out."

"The chambers'll be ready tomorrow afternoon. Come by any time after two."

"Okay, I'll check with Arya. I think we can be there by 2:30." Kaem waited a moment for a response but none came. "Odin, is Mr. Schmidt still on the line?"

"No," Odin replied, "he disconnected immediately after his last words."

Typical, Kaem thought. *Or maybe he was asleep.*

He called Arya.

***

As they rode in the Uber to Schmidt's house, Kaem described how grumpy Gunnar sounded when they'd talked on the phone the night before.

Arya said, "I'll bet you woke him up." She paused for a moment and then said, "Though, maybe he's pissed because I didn't offer him a bigger share of the profits. He is putting up a pretty big stake for all your experiments."

Kaem snorted, "I think he expects to be very satisfied with one percent."

"Really? You think stasis is going to be worth enough that he'd be happy with a piece that small?"

Kaem shrugged, "You're the businessperson. But I think it's going to disrupt almost every industry. Things that do that are usually worth a lot of money"

It was her turn to snort, "There you go being Mr. Optimist again." She shook her head, "I can imagine that, if living organisms aren't damaged by being in stasis, we might have a business model where some people might go into stasis for ten years hoping a cure'll be developed for their untreatable cancer." She made a face, "I guess that'd probably be thousands of people, but I think a lot of people would be worried about popping out of stasis and finding out all their friends

Laurence E Dahners

and relatives are old or dead. Worse, what if one of your relatives spent all your money while you were gone and there's still not a cure? You could find yourself friendless, lonely, broke and *still* dying of cancer."

They were arriving. As Kaem got out of the car, he said, "Trust me, there'll be a lot more uses than just jumping ahead a few years. But even if that were the only thing it was good for, I'll bet there are a bunch of crazy people who'd put themselves in stasis for a thousand years just to see what the future's like."

"What other uses?"

Kaem knocked on the door of Schmidt's shop. He glanced at Arya, "Wait and see, business guru, wait and see."

Arya was saying, "How can I project our business cases if you won't tell me…?" Schmidt pulled the door open and wordlessly waved them in. She gave Kaem a mini glare and said, "Later."

As they walked into Gunnar's workplace the old man eyed the rack of electronics Kaem was carrying. "Well, that's a lot less of a mess than the pile of crap you brought last time. Is it going to work as well?"

"A lot better," Kaem said. "Thanks for financing the upgrade."

"No need to thank me. You're going to pay for it with my piece of the action, remember?"

Kaem said, "Arya thinks you're grumpy because she didn't offer you a bigger piece."

Gunnar glanced at Arya and snorted. "Oh, I'm happy. *She's* clueless." He winked at her, "It's just that this's as sunny as my disposition ever gets."

They spent about half an hour hooking Kaem's new electronics up to the new 15 cm cubical chamber Gunnar'd built.

While they did so, Arya set her phone up on its little mount and positioned it so it'd be able to record video of the chamber.

"We're ready," Kaem said.

"Okay," Arya said, getting out one of the birthday candles and a box of matches. She lit the candle, then held it horizontally in the 15 cm chamber until a bit of wax dripped on the bottom. She stuck the candle into the wax.

"Geez," Gunnar complained, "I *had* it all clean!"

"Yeah, yeah," Arya said backing away and checking the alignment on her phone. She started it recording, then said, "Go ahead."

Gunnar closed and latched the door. "How long are you hoping your stasis is going to last this time?" he asked Kaem.

"A hundred seconds," Kaem said. "One and two-thirds minutes." There was a whine from a charging capacitor, then a snap as it discharged.

"Okay to open the door?" Gunnar asked.

"Sure."

Three sets of eager eyes watched the door open. The candle flickered in the puff of air that resulted. "Crap," Kaem said.

Arya's heart sunk and her thoughts ran. *What if that first stasis field we set up was through some kind of strange serendipity? What if we're never able to form a field again?!*

Why did I spend so much money on this project?!

The two men didn't seem to consider that possibility. They just started troubleshooting. Making sure the laser was coming on when power was supplied. Measuring the RF field in the chamber when the antenna was activated. Kaem started checking all the settings on his electronic gear. Suddenly he said, "Oh. Okay, let's try it again."

"What was it?" Arya asked.

"I'd rather not say," he replied, though Arya thought he looked chagrined, as if he'd made some kind of dumb mistake. "Have you restarted your camera?"

She rolled her eyes. "Okay, restarting now." When it was going she got out another candle.

This time when they opened the door of the chamber they were greeted by the kind of silvery mirrored surface they'd seen the first time. Arya felt her jittery nerves relax and imagined she heard sighs of relief from the two men as well. But it stayed silvery and stayed silvery. "What's happened?" she asked worriedly.

"We're just coming up on the hundred seconds… Now!" Kaem said.

A beat later, the silvery surface disappeared and the candle reappeared, still burning and looking pretty much unchanged. When Arya went back through the video, she could tell a minuscule amount of candle'd been consumed, but she thought it seemed to be about the right amount for the length of time it'd taken to close the door on the chamber and turn on the stasis.

They tried it again with Kaem's watch. It fell behind by exactly the hundred and one seconds that passed between the audible snap of the capacitor when Kaem turned on stasis and the disappearance of the mirrored field on the video. Kaem punched the air excitedly at the confirmation of the accuracy of his new set-up.

They didn't have a mouse but Kaem had brought some crickets one of the girls in his dorm kept to feed her chameleon. They put a cricket in stasis for 100 seconds. When the field collapsed the little guy was immediately walking—as if he'd popped in and out of stasis in midstride and just kept on trucking.

He seemed fine. Arya had the eerie feeling that the cricket didn't even know anything had happened.

Crickets live eight to ten weeks after they reach their adult form, so they put a smaller, presumably younger, cricket in the chamber and set stasis for five megaseconds (58 days). Hopefully, when the stasis collapsed, they'd still have a young cricket. One who'd live for another eight weeks or so—thus proving that stasis hadn't caused it significant harm.

Now came the moment Kaem and Gunnar'd been waiting for. Gunnar tipped the chamber up so the stasis field containing the cricket would fall out of the cavity. They were looking forward to finally seeing a stazed fragment of space-time from all sides.

It didn't fall out.

Gunnar took a deep breath, threw his head back and let out a curse. "I *swear* there's nothing in there for it to hang up on! The walls are perfectly smooth."

Kaem said, "Relax. It's just such a perfect fit air can't get in around it. It's being held in by a vacuum effect. Suction you'd call it."

Gunnar blinked, glanced at the chamber, then said, "Of course it is. I knew that all along. I was just waiting to see if an egghead could figure it out."

Arya snorted, but made no comment.

It took some doing, but once they had a thin blade pushed in so it bowed the mirrored glass wall of the chamber slightly away from the stazed cube, allowing a little air to get in there and break the suction, the frictionless cube practically squirted out of the glass-walled compartment.

It fell very slowly, twisting as it dropped. Something like a feather.

It landed on the concrete floor with a faint muted click. It barely bounced, then slid as frictionlessly across the floor as one might've expected from their findings on that first day. Like a puck in air-hockey. It bounced off the leg of Gunnar's band saw, but the bounce was as weak as the bounce off the floor. It looked like it'd just keep sliding forever, but then Kaem bent down and scooped it up, holding it strangely in cupped hands like you might cradle a frightened animal you expected to try to escape.

Arya asked, "Why'd it fall so funny?"

"It's 6 inches, by 6 inches, by 6 inches," Gunnar said, "but weighs as much as a cricket."

"Wait. It has a bunch of air in it."

"Air that has exactly the same density as the air around it, so it's perfectly buoyant."

"But a balloon only has air in it..." she trailed off.

"Yeah, air under pressure from the elasticity of the balloon, so it's a little heavier than the surrounding air, plus it has the weight of the balloon—which weighs more than our friend the cricket."

"It didn't *bounce* like a balloon," Arya said musingly.

"Nope. It bounces like something really light, yet impossibly hard. It doesn't hit very hard and has absolutely no spring-back. The only springiness to produce a bounce came from the concrete it landed on."

They'd gathered around to stare at the silver cube. It felt like it was hard to see because the only things they saw were reflections off something else. Perfect reflections. Arya reached out and gently felt a corner. "It's rounded," she observed.

"I think that's because the field can't form features under a certain size," Kaem said. "Which is good since then it might've extended little slivers out into any cracks at the joins between the mirrors. That could have made it impossible to get the stade out of the chamber. I was worried it might and that they'd be ultra-sharp, making this thing dangerous to handle."

Gunnar said, "I was worried about that so I was really careful about the joins on this one. It's good to know I don't have to spend so much time in the future."

"Stade?" Arya asked.

Kaem shrugged, "Yeah. We need new words. We've been saying 'stazed when we're talking about how we've put something in stasis. It felt to me like we needed a word for a stazed object so we didn't have to say 'stazed object' all the time."

Arya shrugged, "Okay." She looked thoughtful, "Are you thinking... I'm getting the impression that you think a stazed object, sorry, a stade, may have value in its own right, without even considering the fact that the things inside it are skipping forward in time?"

"Oh, *hell* yes," Gunnar said. "If that stuff's strong enough, frictionless bearings would be worth their weight in gold!"

Kaem shrugged again, "Among other things..."

"For instance..." Gunnar turned to Kaem, "Can we make another stade?"

"Sure," Kaem said, turning to his equipment rack.

Gunnar turned to the chamber. He picked up a small hose from where it lay on the bench and put it in the chamber, closing the door as far as it'd go on the hose. With a reach, he turned the knob on a bottle sitting on the bench. Arya heard the hissing of gas blowing into the chamber. Gunnar turned to Kaem, "Ready?"

Kaem nodded. Gunnar pulled the hose out, shut the door, latched it, and said, "Now."

Arya heard the capacitor snap.

Gunnar rolled the chamber on its back and opened the door. Arya saw the silvery surface of a stade in the opening. Gunnar was already sliding his blade in between the stade and the mirrored wall of the chamber. A moment later, the stade floated out and rose up to bob along against the ceiling. Gunnar turned to look at them with both a raised eyebrow and a grin.

"Helium?" Kaem asked.

Gunnar nodded, a big smile on his face. "We could make blimps! Blimps that don't leak. You probably know helium atoms are so small that they leak right through the walls of balloons. I'll bet helium doesn't leak out of a stade though. How long can you make a stade last?"

Kaem tilted his hand back and forth. "Based on our first test, at least nine days. My theory says we could make them last millions of years, but there's no way to prove that."

Arya stared at Kaem. "Millions of years?! Talk about your non-biodegradable waste! We wouldn't ever try to make one that lasts that long, would we?"

Kaem evenly looked back at her. "Who knows? Let's not get ahead of ourselves. A million-year stade isn't likely, no, but someday there may be a reason to make a few that last nearly that long." He looked at Gunnar. "I think we should get that thing down off the ceiling and restrain it somehow. I'd hate for it to get loose, float up into the atmosphere and get sucked into a jet engine. I have a feeling it'd be pretty destructive."

Gunnar tilted his head back to look at the ceiling. "How would I restrain it?"

"Wrap an old towel around it and tie it in. The towel should be heavy enough to keep it from floating away."

"How long's that one going to last?"

Kaem turned to look at his set up, "One megasecond. Eleven and a half days."

Gunnar looked back up at the ceiling where the stade rested. "I'm not sure how it's going to escape from up there."

Kaem said, "I agree it's probably pretty safe up there... Unless another one of your customers sees it up there and decides to try to take it home with him." He shook his head, "Even if you trust the other people you work with, I don't. If you'd let me borrow a towel, I'll take it with me."

Gunnar shook his head, "No. You've got a point. I'll get a towel and we'll bind it up, but you should think about whether it'll be safer in a closet in my house," he jerked a thumb over his shoulder at his attached home, "or in your dorm where some idiot roommate might decide to borrow your towel. Or just unwrap it to see what you've got tied up."

Kaem snorted, "Your closet it is."

Gunnar headed off into the house to get a towel and some string. Kaem moved the shop's stepladder over underneath the stade and climbed up after it. Arya watched as he carefully surrounded it with the fingers of both hands and used his nails to tilt one edge off the ceiling. Once it was tipped a little bit away, he got his fingers around it and descended the ladder holding it gingerly under an overarching basket of his fingers.

Gunnar returned with a towel and draped it over the stazed cube in Kaem's hands. Once Gunnar had it surrounded by the towel, Kaem slid his hands out. Gunnar pinched the towel in around the bottom of the stade and Kaem tied it with the string Gunnar'd brought. When they were done, it looked a little like a rag doll, but the towel was heavy enough it no longer floated.

Next, they turned their attention to the other chamber Gunnar'd built. This one was 7.5 x 15 cm, but it was only one mm thick. As they were hooking it up, Arya asked, "What's this one for? It doesn't seem like you'd be able to put anything inside it."

Absently, Kaem said, "We wanted a specimen we could use to test the material properties of a stade."

"Oh," Arya said, thinking. "This stuff would make a great frying pan, wouldn't it? *Nothing* would stick to it. It'd be like Teflon on steroids."

"Um," Kaem said, eyeing her with a suppressed grin, "couple problems with that. No friction, remember? Your pan would slide right off the burner unless you held it there."

Arya shrugged, "Attach a frictiony ring around the bottom of it to give it a little traction."

"Frictiony? Now *you're* inventing words! The problem with that is that I don't think we can 'attach' anything to it. Remember how nothing stuck to the first one. Well…" he stared off into the distance, "maybe you could trap your pan in a metal ring that had a rough under surface to provide traction. But then you'd come to problem number two." He arched a questioning eyebrow at her.

She rolled her eyes, "Okay, what's problem number two?"

"I don't think stazed objects are going to transmit heat."

"Oh," Arya said, chagrined. "I can see that. If time isn't passing inside, then there aren't any molecules vibrating with the heat, right?"

He grinned at her, "That's what I'd expect. But as soon as we have our test specimen, we can heat one side of it and see if the other side gets warm." He glanced at Gunnar, "Ready?"

Gunnar nodded.

Arya saw that the door was shut on the compartment. A moment later she heard the snap of capacitor discharge from Kaem's set up.

Gunnar looked at Kaem, "Open it up?"

Kaem nodded.

Gunnar undid the latch, then said, "Oh-oh."

Sounding anxious, Kaem said, "What's wrong?"

He and Arya converged on the thin chamber. It took Arya a moment to recognize there was an irregular hole in the middle of the 7.5 x 15 cm mirrored sheet. It was a little hard to see the hole because the mirror lining the chamber was right behind it.

Arya asked, "You think you need to give it more power?"

Kaem shook his head. "I don't think it's a power issue. I think it's the same thing that makes a staze have rounded corners. We can't staze a segment of space-time with a dimension smaller than about one mm, at least not with our current setup. This chamber's supposed to be a millimeter thick, but I'll bet the middle of it's just a tiny bit thinner. Just barely thin enough that some areas weren't thick enough to staze."

While they'd been talking, Gunnar'd hooked a fingernail in the hole in the middle of the silvery plate and lifted it out of the chamber. He waved it at them, "Hey, if you're done jawing, I'd like to point out that having a hole in this thing makes it a lot easier to handle."

Kaem made a face, "Easy to handle, but its irregular shape makes it a lot harder to use as a mechanical test sample."

Gunnar shrugged, "I agree, it's not the kind of specimen we'd want to send to the lab for definitive testing, but it'll take me a few days to make a chamber that's a tiny bit thicker. In the meantime, we can heat this one to see if it melts, breaks, or resists the transmission of heat. We can hit it with a hammer and see if it's strong. We can get *some* idea of what to expect."

Kaem said, "I'll bet if you put a tiny shim under the edges of the door, thus propping it open just a little, we'll still form a staze, this time one that's a tiny bit thicker and doesn't have a hole in the middle of it."

Gunnar got a thoughtful look and said, "Right, because if we prop the door open less than a millimeter, the field that forms the stade won't leak out the gap. Or something like that, right?"

Kaem nodded, "Something like that."

"Let's see if we can break this one then, okay?"

Kaem nodded. Then, when Gunnar turned and put the thin plate between the jaws of a heavy-duty vice, he grinned and said, "Ah, this should be interesting."

For a moment Arya wondered what Kaem thought would be interesting.

Gunnar finished tightening the vice on the thin plate, then turned and walked to the corner to get his torch.

Arya immediately saw what Kaem thought would be interesting. Though Gunnar'd cranked the vice down hard, the little plate just slipped out of its grip and floated away. *Actually,* she thought, *it didn't "slip" out.*

It's more as if it got squirted out like a watermelon seed. Probably the jaws weren't quite parallel because the stade was holding that end of the gap open. Then they squirted that frictionless plate right out of there. She grinned, looking at the plate slowly tumbling through the air. *And, because its only weight comes from the stazed air that was in the chamber, the stade itself floats in the room's atmosphere.*

Gunnar returned, dragging a small cart with an oxy-acetylene torch. He blinked at the empty vice, then saw the plate, still rotating in midair a little way from the vice. He snorted and shook his head. "Damn, this's hard to get used to." Snatching the stade out of the air, he walked over to his trashcan and pulled out a wad of rusty steel wool. He stuffed the wool into the hole in the middle of the stade plate. This time when he closed the vice on it, the crushed wool in the irregular hole kept the plate from sliding around.

Gunnar turned on the acetylene and struck a spark in front of the torch. Without turning on the oxygen, he played the torch over the stade plate for about ten seconds, then holding the torch off to one side he licked a finger and touched the plate.

Arya listened for the slight pop and hiss of saliva boiling against something hot. She didn't hear anything.

Gunnar shook his head and put his finger back on the plate. Turning to the other two, he gave a little laugh and said, "Feels warm... Body-temperature warm. Same as these damn things feel when you *haven't* played a torch over them."

He turned on some oxygen and adjusted the flame to a sharp blue point. Lifting his goggles up over his eyes, he played the point on the plate for about a minute. Arya noticed some of the steel wool that stuck up out of the vice was turning red and sparking, suggesting he'd delivered some serious heat. Gunnar turned the torch away, dropped the goggles, then bent his knees so he could study the stade plate with the lower lenses of his bifocals. "Damn! That would've melted steel, but this little mirror still looks completely unblemished." Again he wet a fingertip and touched the plate, then pinched it between his fingers. Shaking his head in amazement, he said, "And not a *damned* bit warmer."

Kaem turned to grin at Arya, "I guess we won't be making your frying pans."

She gently slugged his shoulder, "Wise ass."

Gunnar turned off the torch and said, "I want to hit it with a hammer. Any other rough and ready tests you want to do before I try to break it?"

"No," Kaem said slowly.

"You sound like you're thinking of something?"

Kaem shook his head, "Just trying to make sure we haven't missed some reason why hitting it with a hammer might be dangerous. I can't think of one, but why don't you put a big crescent wrench on it and try to bend it first?"

"Good idea," Gunnar said, pulling a large crescent wrench off a wall hook and adjusting it until it fit snugly over the 1 mm plate. Then he leaned on it, trying to bend the plate. Arya couldn't see any deformation in the plate. A few moments later Gunnar grabbed the wrench with both hands and leaned his whole body into it.

The wrench slipped off.

Gunnar nearly fell, but caught himself. "Damned thing keeps catching me by surprise," he said, shaking his head morosely, though he had a little grin. He picked a ball-peen hammer off his wall rack. "Maybe it's brittle. Let's see how it responds to a sudden shock."

Kaem said, "Hit it gently the first time, okay?"

"Sure," Gunnar said. He tapped one side of the plate, then slowly increased the velocity of his swings until he was hitting it hard. He shook his head. "The sound it makes is so weird. You might get that kind of dull click from soft metal, but it would've bent when I hit it. Metal hard enough to make the hammer bounce back like this should ring, sounding a little bit like a bell." He glanced at them, "Though the hammer doesn't bounce back like it should."

Kaem said, "A stade isn't springy. At all. Therefore, no ringing like a bell, no bouncing back other than the springiness of the hammer's head and any recoil coming out of the vice and bench."

"Can I hit it harder?"

"Sure, but increase the force a little at a time so we don't run into any weird surprises, okay?"

Gunnar hit it a solid blow with pretty much the same results they'd had before. A little louder click, a slightly stronger bounce back, a little shaking of items on the bench the vice was attached to. He took a big swing and hit it really hard with no more effect, other than on bench items shaken by the blow transmitted through the vice. He hung the ball peen hammer back up and grabbed a sledgehammer.

"Whoa," Kaem said. "You should have on your safety glasses, shouldn't you?"

Gunnar rolled his eyes, but pulled out a drawer that contained several sets of safety glasses. He put on a pair and handed sets to Kaem and Arya. This time he took a mighty swing with the sledge. He got the same result as when he hit it with the smaller hammer, just more shaking of the bench on the tools on it. He hung up the sledge, took off the safety glasses, and stared at the slender plate. "Wow!"

Kaem said, "I need to get back pretty soon to meet with some other students on a project. Can you try to shim the door open a tiny bit so we can see if we can make a few complete plates? I want to take some samples to a testing lab I found. You can keep this one with the hole in it and keep trying to break it if you want."

Gunnar put some thin flat pieces of metal he called "feeler gauges" between the chamber and the door then latched it. Kaem fired off his electronics and Gunnar levered a complete plate out with his knife.

When Gunnar was passing it to Kaem it slipped loose and floated off through the air. Kaem stared at it for a moment, then said, "Can you put something heavy in the next one so our test versions won't be so light? I don't want to weird out the test lab when we take them in for testing. Their properties are going to be hard enough to believe without the test people wondering how they can be as light as air."

Gunnar scratched his head. "You want me to cut a piece of sheet metal almost big enough to fill the cavity?"

"No…" Kaem said, pausing to think. "A big piece of metal might cause problems with reflections of the radar waves." He blinked, "Oh, hell, we need to find out whether that's true. It'd just as well be now."

Gunnar used his tin snips to cut a piece of aluminum flashing 7 cm x 14.5 cm. As he started to lay it in the chamber, he said, "Obviously it's going to be touching on the bottom. There'll be some places where it'll stick out of the surface of the stasis field."

"Shouldn't matter," Kaem said. "*Everything* inside the field goes into stasis. Once it's stazed it should look and act the same as the air in the chamber." He tilted his head curiously, "Well, except for the way it reacts to gravity."

"You're probably right," Gunnar said, carefully positioning the plate so it was centered. He closed the lid and latched it. Once Kaem fired off his electronics, Gunnar tipped the chamber over and opened the lid. This stade fell out under its own weight. It skidded across the bench and fell to the floor, skittering under the base of an arc welder. When Kaem managed to trap and pick it up, he said, "This feels a lot better." He turned it over. "There's no evidence of the spots where the plate was touching the bottom of the chamber. Looks like, except for mass, one thing in stasis *is* just like another, all mirror."

"I think they're going to be freaked out enough by its frictionless surfaces, infinite insulation value, and impossible strength." Gunnar laughed, "'Light as air' wouldn't have been a major issue."

Kaem had developed a frown.

Gunnar laughed, "What now?"

"I've started wondering... They're going to be doing all these precision measurements. What if they detect differential density across the stade?"

"Differential density?"

"Yeah, because the metal plate might have wound up a tiny bit off-center. I don't know if they'll be doing any tests that notice it's a little heavier on one side than another, but that could confuse the whole issue of its properties. Is there a way we could distribute the weight more precisely?"

"I could try to cut a plate that fills the cavity?"

"Cutting it by hand might be a problem all by itself, don't you think?"

"Put matching washers in each corner?"

Arya said, "Level up the chamber and pour water in it."

Kaem shook his head, "We'd wind up with an air bubble on the top surface. It'd tend to always float with that side up."

Gunnar laughed, "They'd have a hard time telling that, since they can't mark one side to tell which one's up. But, if we fill the chamber carefully, surface tension will make it bulge up. When we close the door on top of it, the extra water'll squeeze out and we should get a stade that's completely filled with water."

They tried it and it appeared to work. To confirm there weren't any bubbles inside the stade, they dropped it in a bucket of water. Once it plunged in, it stayed underwater and didn't seem to prefer floating with any side or corner up. "It's got to be completely full of water," Gunnar concluded.

"Damn, I'm going to be late for my meeting!" Kaem said.

Arya called an Uber while they were making a couple more water-filled stades.

As they opened the door to head out to the car, Gunnar shook Kaem's hand. "I'm not sure exactly what you've got here, but, *damn*!"

They rode back to the University in silence. Arya thought they were both trying to come to grips with what it all meant.

Chapter Five

At Harris Laboratories

Raymond looked up when Cathy knocked on the door frame. She said, "I've got a guy here who wants to hand-deliver some test specimens."

"We're not going to get to them for at least a week."

"I told him that. He wants to talk to someone about what kind of tests he'd like run."

"Just tell him to pick his tests from the list," Raymond said, irritated.

"He says he wants to know whether the specimens he brought are the right kind for testing. If they aren't, he could be preparing something different during the week he has to wait."

Well, that's interesting, Raymond thought. *People were always delivering untestable specimens and then wanting to know why the lab couldn't magically define all their properties anyway.* "Okay, bring the guy back."

Cathy returned with a skinny looking black kid in his early 20s. Obviously the delivery boy, not someone who'd understand testing. "What do they want us to test?"

"Something new," the kid said, pulling a couple of 5 x 7 manila envelopes out of a bigger envelope.

"Nothing new under the sun, sonny," Raymond quipped.

The kid shrugged. Undoing the flap on an envelope, he tilted it and carefully caught what looked like a 3" x 6" mirror as it slid out into his other hand. He caught it so it sloped down into his hand, hooking on the middle three fingers and restrained on each side by the thumb and small finger.

That's a beautiful mirror, Raymond thought, reaching for it.

"Careful," the kid said, "it's pretty much frictionless."

Raymond had grasped the end that was sticking up out of the kid's hand, gripping it from edge to edge because he thought the kid was holding it gingerly to keep from getting the surface smudged. But when he tried to pull the mirror up out of the kid's hand, his fingers just slipped off. He blinked, startled, then pushed his reading glasses up his nose and leaned down for a closer look. *It's pretty much a perfect mirror,* he thought, realizing he couldn't actually see the mirror, only the things reflected in it.

Straightening up, he said, "I'll be damned if it *isn't* something new. What kind of tests do you want run on it?"

"Coefficient of friction—"

"Friction against what?" Raymond interrupted, "A coefficient's meaningless unless you define what it's sliding against."

"Against anything. We think its coefficient's going to be zero against *any* substance, but if you find something it gets traction on, we'd surely like to know that."

Raymond snorted, "No such thing as a coefficient of zero."

The kid shrugged, "Then please, measure it for us. We'd love to have a measured value… We'd also like to know its thermal resistance."

"You mean heat transmission?"

The kid nodded. "And, we'd like to know how well it blocks radiation."

"What kind of radiation?"

He shrugged, "Alpha, beta, gamma, neutrons, cosmic, x-rays; whatever you can test it against, we'd like the results."

Raymond grunted, surprised at the depth of the kid's knowledge. *Maybe he isn't just the delivery boy?* "We can test everything but cosmic."

"Great!" The kid said, sounding pleased. "And we'd also like mechanical properties testing."

Raymond looked at the little mirror. "Can I touch the face of it? Or is that going to mess up the mirrored surface?"

"Go ahead."

Raymond grabbed it from flat surface to flat surface, intending to slide it off the kid's hand, but his fingers slid right off again. He tried gripping it harder, but still couldn't hold it well enough to pull it off the kid's hand.

The kid shrugged, "Pretty close to frictionless. If you'll grab it again, I'll try to tip my side up so gravity'll push it into your hand, but it's still going to try to slide out either side unless you trap it with your fingers like I'm doing."

Simply unable to believe what the kid said, Raymond nodded, pinched it from flat surface to flat surface, and waited while the kid tipped his hand up so that gravity was pushing it through his pinching fingers and into his palm.

The kid said, "Ready?"

Raymond wanted to say, "Of course," but with the kid having been proven right so many times already, he just nodded. The kid let go and for a second, Raymond thought he had it, but then it slipped to his left and vanished from his hand. Bizarrely, Raymond couldn't even feel it sliding. It fell through the air, barely

Laurence E Dahners

bounced off the concrete floor, slid over and bounced even less off the leg of their small hydraulic materials testing machine, then slowly slid under a cabinet. Raymond thought he was going to have to try to snag it out from under the cabinet with a wire. He picked up a spool of stiff wire and stepped that way, but when he arrived, the little mirror came sliding very slowly out on its own. *An even weaker bounce back from under the bench,* Raymond thought. He bent over to grab it.

The kid said, "Put your fingers on all four sides of it or it'll get away. Then work a fingernail under it on one side to lift that edge enough to pick it up."

Raymond wanted to tell the kid he was smart enough to figure that out, but in fact, he'd been wondering how to do it. Rather than embarrass himself further, he picked up the reflective plate as he'd been instructed. He turned and said, "If we can't grip it, we can't do tensile testing."

"Yeah, it seems like we'd have to get you a massively narrowed dog-bone specimen with really big shoulders you could hook around. When the time comes to do that test perhaps you could advise us on the best shape?"

"Or a specimen with threaded ends."

The kid looked thoughtful for a moment, then said, "I think we should start with a three-point bending test on the plate you've got. We could infer tensile strength from that."

"Or, if you like, we could cut sections out of either side of the plate you've given us. Make our own dog-bone testing specimen to hook onto."

The kid said, "After you've done everything else, you're welcome to try. I'm afraid it might be really hard to cut."

"Laser cutter, plasma torch. We'll find something that'll cut it."

"If you try it, be careful. I think it'll reflect the beam back onto your cutter."

Raymond's eyes went back to the perfect mirrored surface of the specimen. He noticed it didn't even have fingerprints from when he'd grabbed it. *Can it possibly reflect so much of the beam it won't be damaged itself?* he wondered. "Okay, a three-point bending test it is. Any other tests you want done?"

"We'd like it if you *could* find a way to break, cut, or otherwise damage or destroy it."

"That should be easy," Raymond said. "Since we don't have a charge for just trying to break something, we'll just continue the bending test until failure. Any other testing?"

The kid shook his head.

"We won't be getting to it for a week or so," Raymond lied. "Stop off at Cathy's desk and fill out the paperwork. Tick the checkboxes for all the tests we've just discussed. She'll give you a price. I'm afraid you'll have to prepay; we've had some deadbeats."

"No problem," the kid said and turned for the door.

As he left Raymond heard him telling his phone to call for an Uber. *A messenger that doesn't even have a car?* Raymond tipped the specimen back into its envelope, then turned to finish the test he'd been working on when he'd been interrupted. He wanted to be sure the kid was out of the building before he actually started testing the specimen. *But I've got to see what the deal is with this thing!*

Everyone else's tests can wait.

***

James Harris looked up on hearing someone clear their throat. Raymond Weldon stood in his doorway. "What's up?" Harris asked.

Weldon said, "You said you wanted to know if anybody brought truly unusual specimens in for testing?"

"Uh-huh."

"Well, a few days ago we got two of the weirdest damned specimens I've ever seen."

Harris looked down at what he'd been working on. It could wait. Feeling a surge of anticipation, he stood and said, "Let's go look at it."

As he followed Weldon back to the testing lab Harris wondered whether the specimen might represent some new and exotic material. It'd be especially great if it was some new material that might have significant commercial value. Though his company was doubtlessly restrained from telling anyone about the material—by its own nondisclosure rule if nothing else—that didn't mean Harris's shell company couldn't quietly buy some stock in the company that invented it.

A minute or so later, he was carefully holding a 7.5 x 15 cm mirror. It was very thin; Harris would've estimated about a millimeter. Raymond confirmed that, measured with a caliper, it was 1.1 mm. It was weird to look at because it was such a *perfect* mirror. You never really saw it, only the things it reflected. The most visible parts of it were the rounded edges where the reflected objects were so markedly reduced in size by the convexity of the reflective surface that it gave the impression of a line.

Just the way it slid around on his fingers made Harris believe Raymond's assertion that he couldn't measure any static friction. Raymond had said, "Hell, I can't get our test platform level enough to keep it from sliding away in one direction or another. And, putting weight on it to increase the friction doesn't slow it down either.

Harris said its density was 1 gram per cc, same as water. Getting its weight was difficult because of its tendency to slide off the scale, but Harris had fixed that by putting it in a large tare dish. Measuring its volume wasn't simple because of its rounded edges. When Harris had tried to measure volume by water displacement, he'd found that the little mirror didn't float or sink—also suggesting its density was the same as the water it was displacing.

"So," Harris said, "if its coefficient of friction is so close to zero we can't measure it, it'd make a great bearing material. Well, that's if it's strong enough. Hell, if it's strong enough, railroad cars could be mounted on sliders instead of wheels."

"That'd be fine until you needed to put on the brakes," Raymond said.

Harris laughed, "I guess you're right. They'd have to have a second set of skids they lowered when they wanted to stop. For a second there I'd been thinking we could mount cars and airplanes on skids as well, but I suppose they'd slide sideways just as well as they do forward, huh?" He snorted, "*That'd* be a problem." He lifted his eyes back to Raymond, "*Is* it strong enough to make a bearing material out of it?"

"Boss, this part's even harder to believe. I loaded that little plate in your hand in three-point bending. If there *was* any deflection, it was within the measurement error of the machine. I don't think it deformed at all."

"Wait a minute," Harris said feeling a little irritated, "There must have been a problem with the measurement of displacement. Did it *look* deformed?"

Raymond slowly shook his head.

"So, you're saying that even at max load..." He looked over at their medium material tester. "What's the maximum load the machine can produce, 500 pounds?"

Raymond nodded, "Close. The medium-sized machine you're looking at goes up to 2000 N which is pretty close to 450 pounds. But boss, when I didn't get any inflection on that one, I went to the big one. It goes to ten metric tons. That damned little plate still didn't fail! That means it has a flexural strength of at least 260,000 megapascals, hundreds of times stronger than structural steel. Graphene's supposed to be the world's strongest material and they *think* it has a tensile strength half that. Unfortunately, nobody's ever been able to make a big enough piece of graphene to test. This is at least that strong, probably a lot stronger since there wasn't any displacement."

"You didn't get deformation at ten metric tons?!"

Raymond slowly shook his head. "At those kinds of loads the machine's straining so hard there's some jitter in the data so we can't be *sure* it didn't deform a little," Raymond's eyes went to the thin mirror in Harris's hand, "but I'd swear it didn't."

"Holy shit!" Harris said slowly, "So, if it can be formed into a reasonable shape, it's essentially the ultimate bearing material, huh?" He looked at Raymond, "You think they can make bigger pieces of it? Structural members for, say, a building?"

"I have no idea. They brought us two plates that seem like they're exactly alike. Maybe this is the only shape they can make. Maybe they just found these two plates somewhere and brought them in, hoping our tests would tell them what they were."

"What're they made of?"

Raymond produced a caricature-like shrug of his shoulders. "Lord only knows! The guy that brought the specimens didn't say."

"Have you tried spectroscopy?"

"Yeah, that's another thing. Anything you beam at it gets reflected. Perfectly. 100% reflected. The beam from the spectroscope comes back absolutely unchanged."

"'Anything' reflects?"

"Alpha, beta, and gamma particles. Neutrons. X-rays, UV, visible light, radar on down through radio... *Everything* just bounces off, including the electron gun we used to determine the melting and vaporization temperatures of refractory materials."

"So we couldn't determine the melting temperature either?!"

Raymond shook his head, "I'm sure you know we normally use the electron gun or induction heating of *tiny* specimens to determine the heat tolerance of a material. Since I couldn't cut a tiny specimen off, I put the whole thing in our research furnace for four hours, but it only goes up to 3,000°C. That's 5,430°F, not even hot enough to melt tungsten."

"Did it even get red-hot?"

"No," Raymond said, staring at the little mirror as if he still didn't believe the results. "You probably won't believe this, but when I got it out of the furnace it wasn't even hot."

"What do you mean?! Are you saying it didn't get up to—?"

"I mean I could handle it with my bare fingers as soon as I took it out of the furnace. Have you noticed how it feels warm?"

Harris looked down at where it rested in his hand, "It does, doesn't it?"

"It *always* feels that temperature. No matter what I've been doing to it. But if you shoot it with an infrared thermometer? The thermal gun thinks it's at room temperature. I get the same thing with a thermocouple thermometer *and* the same thing with mercury or alcohol thermometers." Raymond snorted, "The damned thermometers feel *cool* to my fingers. I *just don't* get it!"

"My God!" Harris said racking his brain for how Raymond could be getting such bizarre answers. It made him want to repeat the tests himself, but he was honest enough to know that, though he might own the company, Raymond was much better at performing the actual testing than he was. "Thanks for bringing this to my attention."

Raymond shrugged. "You wanted to know about any crazy specimens."

"You bet I did, and there'll be a bonus in your check for calling me about this one." Harris looked Raymond in the eye, "For God's sake, don't tell anyone else about this, okay?"

Raymond nodded again.

"What company sent these things in?"

"The kid that delivered it didn't say. Hopefully, Cathy's got it on the intake form. At a minimum, she should have some kind of contact info so we'd be able to send them their results."

"I'll check. You've finished your testing?"

Curtis tilted his head. "Pretty much. He said I could cut it into a dog bone shape for tensile testing and that they'd like it if we could test it to destruction. The problem is I can't find anything that'll cut it, or break it, or damage it in *any* way, much less destroy it."

Harris racked his brain. "How about if you loaded it in axial compression?"

Raymond said, "I thought of that. Here's the problem. The compressive strength of steel's only about 150 megapascals." He shook his head, "Hard to believe I'm saying 'only...' Ten metric tons of pressure on a 7.5 square millimeter surface would be 13,400 megapascals. Remember, we measured the bending strength of that plate and it's at *least* 260,000 megapascals." He nodded at the plate in Harris's hand, "Bending puts compression on the material on one side and tension on the other, so, that thing can't be much weaker in compression than it is in bending. If we try to test it in compression it's just going to slice into whatever fixture we try to apply the compression with." He glanced at the mirror, "It'll cut steel the way a hot knife cuts butter."

Harris stared at the little mirror for about thirty seconds, then said, "Damn!" He shook his head, "If I think of something to try, I'll let you know." He headed down the hall.

Stepping into Cathy's office he said, "I need the contact info for the company that delivered the specimens Raymond's been working on."

Before Cathy could find the correct intake paperwork, they had to check with Raymond to get the date the specimens had been delivered.

When she handed the sheet over, Harris felt a twinge of dismay. The blank for "company" hadn't been filled in. He looked at Cathy "Um, the company name's blank?"

Cathy looked up and saw the empty blank Harris had his finger on. "Um, right. That's not one of our required pieces of data."

Harris said, "I'd really like to know who's manufacturing those specimens. Can you call and ask politely? You know, say we're just finishing up our paperwork?"

"Sure, Mr. Harris."

***

When Kaem got the call, he was pleased to hear from his AI, Odin, that it was coming from Harris Laboratories. *Maybe they've finished their testing early?* he hoped. But he was in class and didn't want to step out to answer during the lecture.

He called back when his class was over. "Cathy? This is Kaem Seba. You called?" He had his fingers crossed, hoping for results.

"Um, yes. I've been, uh, trying to complete our paperwork. You forgot to fill in the blank for "company" on our intake form? If you'll just tell me who manufactured the specimens, I can fill it in for you."

Damn! Kaem thought, disappointed. To Cathy, he said, "It's a private source, not a company. Your website doesn't say you have any rules against performing testing for individuals."

After a moment's hesitation, Cathy said, "Oh no, that's fine. It's just that... Almost all our testing's done for small to medium companies. I just thought you must've forgotten to fill that blank. Sorry to have bothered you."

"No problem," Kaem said, telling Odin to disconnect. He turned back to his studies, but about ten minutes later, he wondered, *What if they're trying to find out the company because the results are weird?* He pondered this for a minute, then thought, *I'm being paranoid!* He went back to studying.

***

Cathy rapped on his door frame. Harris looked up, "What'd you find out?"

She shook her head, "He says the specimens don't belong to a company. They come from some private individual."

"Him?" Harris looked at the copy he'd made of the intake sheet. "This 'Kaem Seba' person?"

"Um, he didn't say. Do you want me to call him back?"

"No..." Harris sighed, "No, we'd better not kick that sleeping dog again."

Once Cathy left, Harris googled Kaem Seba. Fortunately, the name Seba was uncommon in the States, though there were a lot of people with that name in Africa. The only one nearby was a mixed-race physics student at UVA. *Could some professor in the physics department have created those mirrors? If so, you'd think they'd be doing the testing in the university's facilities... Maybe,* he thought, *some professor's going to try to claim he didn't invent it at the University because if he did UVA would own a big chunk of the rights. Or,* Harris wondered, *could they have* found *those mirrors somewhere? After a few minutes thought, Harris decided "finding them" sounded more like an archaeology department discovery than a physics department invention.*

So, he wondered, *what do I do? It doesn't sound like I can just invest in the company that invented them. But, assuming they can make more of that stuff, and especially if they can make it in other shapes, it's going to be worth a fortune!*

Harris didn't want to miss that ride.

After extensive thought, Harris decided he was going to have to try to talk to this Kaem Seba. Talking to a college student sounded like a waste of his time, but if he applied enough grease to the kid's palm, he should be able to find out where the plates came from.

That wasn't a task he could delegate to someone else.

Chapter Six

Encountering James Harris

Kaem and Arya were eating lunch together. She asked, "What do you think our first product should be?"

"I don't know. There're so many possibilities it's hard to choose."

"We can't build them all. In fact, it'll be hard to set up even *one* product for serious manufacturing with Gunnar as our only investor."

Kaem gave a little laugh. "I hope you're not going to tell me you want to sell stock?"

"Not yet, but we might have to."

"What *are* you thinking?"

"That we might be able to do it ourselves if we start with a really high-value product. One that's not too expensive or difficult for us to make." She glanced distractedly across the room and twirled a hank of hair around a finger. "Something with a high enough payoff that we could use *that* money to set up a real manufacturing facility."

"We need the results from the testing," Kaem sighed. "If the strength and heat resistance are as high as I think they'll be; we should be able to build rocket engines. Currently, those are really expensive to make because of the need for exotic alloys to keep the engine from melting when you fire it. Their designs are made much more complex because of the need to pump cold fuel through the rocket engine and nozzle to keep even

Laurence E Dahners

those exotic high-temperature alloys from melting. If we could mold our mirrors…" he trailed off.

"What?"

"Just realizing that we couldn't get our mirrors back out of the combustion chamber because the opening's narrow. We'd have to break them or melt them out." He shrugged, "Presumably, that's not a problem. We probably *couldn't* hurt the inside of the combustion chamber with either explosive fragmentation or high heat melting solutions for removing the mirrors. It's just that it'll increase our costs to have to make a new set of mirrors for each engine."

"What if we made a couple more 7.5 cm x 15 cm test samples and sent them to Space-Gen? They're going to want to do their own tests on the material anyway." Arya broke off at the worried look on Kaem's face. "What's the matter?"

"I've just been realizing there're people out there who might want to steal this from us."

"Oh." She narrowed her eyes, "Anything in particular making you worried? Or just the fact that stade's going to be really valuable?"

"I got a call yesterday from Harris Laboratories, the people that're doing our testing?"

Arya nodded, "What'd they want?"

"I think it was their admin that called. She said she'd noticed I hadn't filled one of the blanks on their specimen intake form. Implied she was just dotting her I's and crossing her T's."

"So?"

"The blank was the one for 'company name.' Because I didn't want to fill that one, I specifically remember that it didn't have an asterisk identifying it as a blank that *had* to be filled in."

Arya studied him for a moment, "And you're thinking someone there wants to know where the test samples came from?"

Kaem nodded.

"What'd you tell her?"

"I told her the specimens came from a private individual and pointed out that their website indicated they do testing for individuals, not just companies."

Arya grinned, "Just not that the private individual was *you*, huh?"

Kaem nodded slowly.

Arya gave a little shrug, "It's probably innocent."

Kaem's phone rang. He turned the display to Arya. It said, "Harris Laboratories."

"Are you going to answer it? she asked.

"I pretty much have to," he said unhappily. "We want the results we paid for, right?" He told the phone to connect Arya's earbud into the call, then answer. "Hello?"

"Hi, is this… Kaem Seba?"

"Yes," Kaem said, trying not to sound suspicious.

"Jim Harris here, owner of Harris Laboratories?"

"Uh, yes, sir Mr. Harris. What can I do for you?"

"You brought in some test specimens earlier this week."

"Yes, sir. Are the results ready?" Kaem put excitement in his tone. He felt certain the results wouldn't be ready, but didn't want to give the man any inkling of his suspicions.

"Oh, no. Still, a lot of work to do there. But I've gotten pretty interested in those specimens. Where'd they come from?"

Laurence E Dahners

"Um," Kaem said uncertainly. "I'm supposed to keep that confidential. Your website says you'll keep it confidential too, right?"

Harris gave a little laugh. One that sounded too hearty for the situation, Kaem thought. Harris said, "Of course, of course. Any chance you and I could meet? Just talk about it a little? I could make it worth your while."

"Oh, no," Kaem said, trying to sound mildly shocked. "I'd be afraid I might give something away. I *promised* to keep all this completely confidential and I wouldn't want to break that promise... Um, do you know when our results will be ready?" He winced.

"Sometime next week," Harris said. "We're still doing some analyses."

"Okay," Kaem said, "thanks. I'll check with Cathy next week then." He had Odin disconnect, wanting to get off the line before Harris could pursue any other angles.

Arya looked worried. "Why'd you wince?"

"I called them 'our results,'" Kaem said. "I hope he didn't notice."

Arya shrugged, "I didn't notice it."

"But you *know* they're our results."

"You need a patent," Arya said. "And a bodyguard."

Kaem snorted, "I'm pretty sure those are both really expensive. A little beyond the means of a dirt poor student."

She got a serious look. "Let's talk to Schmidt. Maybe he'll finance the patent."

"So, we'd put all three of our names on it?"

She frowned, "I looked this up. Only the person who *actually* invented it is supposed to get their name on the patent." Kaem started to protest but she put her hand up to stop him, "Wait. According to my reading, it's simpler if *you* get the patent but assign it to our company, Staze. Then we each share in the profits from the patent the same way we share in Staze."

"And you think Gunnar'd go for that? His share in the company's so small."

"Yeah, he thinks the profits from Staze are going to be huge. He doesn't think it matters how small a piece he has, he's still going to be wealthier than he ever dreamed."

"Okay, but do you mind asking him? I'd be embarrassed."

"Sure, I'll call him... Look, I don't think we should ask Schmidt to hire you a bodyguard, but I don't think you should go places without me."

"What, *you're* gonna protect me?"

She stared at him steadily.

Kaem blinked, "I guess you already did, right? The day we met and you took down that bully."

"Yeah," she winked, "I'm a lot meaner than I look."

Kaem felt uncomfortable. "I don't think you should be trying to protect me. If... if we run into some really bad guy..." he shook his head, "I wouldn't want you risking your life. Better to just tell him how to make stades."

"Maybe," she said, then gave him a sharp look, "but *don't* get all paternalistic on me. I'll make my own decisions."

Kaem put his hands up in surrender, "No problem. *Not* paternalistic. No male chauvinist pigs here." He grinned at her, "Besides, I'm getting to where I kind of like having you around."

She narrowed her eyes, "Is that some kind of sexist comment?"

He put his arms straight up as if he were in a bank robbery, "No, no, no, no! Not sexist! Just thinking of you as a good buddy! The kind of friend I like to hang around with!"

She closed her eyes and pinched the bridge of her nose, muttering, "Are baap re."

"What's that mean?" Kaem asked, suspiciously.

"Hindi for something like, 'Oh my God,'" Arya said, as if she were in pain. "Mom says it all the time. I'm not exactly sure of the translation, but…"

Kaem eyed her, wondering. He teased her a lot, and she sometimes teased him back, but if he said something implying that he liked her she usually cut him off. Suddenly he couldn't take it, "Are your parents arranging your marriage?"

Her eyes flashed back open to stare at him. "Where's *that* coming from?!"

He shrugged sullenly, "I don't know. But isn't that the way it's done in India?"

"I've never lived in India!"

"Well, yeah, but it's your heritage, isn't it?"

"Yeah, but my heritage's none of your business, is it?" she snapped.

Kaem put his hands up again, "Okay, okay. You *be* my bodyguard. I'll try to *not* like having you around. Business partners only."

She gave him a surly look, "We can be friends."

Kaem gave her his best smile, "I'd like that."

Shaking her head, she rolled her eyes.

They got up and started toward the door. Outside, he turned toward his dorm. To his surprise, Arya turned with him. "Where are you going?"

"With you. Bodyguard, remember?" she said, pulling out her phone.

While she mumbled some commands to it, Kaem said, "You don't have to start now, do you? I mean, I was thinking you were just going to bodyguard me when I left campus. That wouldn't be too difficult since I hardly ever go anywhere."

Arya said, "You have a boyfriend in his 50s?"

"Um, no," Kaem said, puzzled.

"There was a guy who came in right before we left. Looked around, then stared at you. After that, he glanced at you several times a minute. You never noticed?"

"No…" Kaem said slowly. "I'm not usually trying to figure out whether guys are staring at me or not. I'm not interested."

"Oh, shit!" Arya said.

"What?"

She held up her phone where he could see the screen. It had a picture of a guy in his 50s with buzz cut reddish hair.

"That's him? You took a picture?"

"That's him, yes. And, no, I didn't take a picture. This is James Harris, CEO of Harris Laboratories."

Kaem swallowed. "Crap!"

Arya stopped and looked in a store window.

Surprised, Kaem looked in the window to see what'd caught her eye. It had a lot of UVA gear, but he'd never seen Arya wearing that kind of paraphernalia. He looked at her. Her head was facing into the store, but her eyes were turned off to the left. *She's looking at a reflection in the window,* he thought, starting to turn left as well. Before he'd rotated more than a few degrees, she grabbed his arm and turned him to the right. With a sharp tug, she started them off down the sidewalk in the same direction they'd been going. She linked her arm in his as if she were his girlfriend.

Suddenly, Kaem got it. "Harris's following us, isn't he?" he asked quietly.

"Yes," she said. "It's not much farther to your dorm. If he follows us all the way there, we can talk to him in the lobby. Aren't there usually a lot of people in there?"

"Yeah, it's a hangout. I suppose I shouldn't turn around and look at him?"

"No, I don't want to give him a chance to call out and try to get us to stop and talk to him here."

Is it wrong for me to enjoy having her hold my arm even if she doesn't want to do it? Kaem wondered.

Right after they entered the lobby of Kaem's dorm the door opened again. Kaem glanced that way and saw a fiftyish man with short red hair coming in. The man's eyes fell on Kaem and widened with false surprise. "Mr. Seba?" the man said, striding toward him.

Kaem glanced at Arya and she gave him a tiny nod. He turned back toward Harris, "Yes?"

The man extended his hand, "Jim Harris. We spoke on the phone just a little while ago."

Kaem reluctantly shook the man's hand. "Yes?"

"I just wanted to..." Harris looked around, "Can we just sit over here? I'd love to just talk to you for a few minutes."

"Um, I'd rather not—"

"Oh, come on," the man said jovially. "I *just* want to talk. Nothing painful." His hand dipped into his pants pocket and he pulled out a twenty-dollar bill. Extending it, he said, "I'll *pay* for the privilege."

Kaem stared at the bill, wanting the money, but not wanting to talk.

The man bobbed it up and down.

Kaem shook his head, "No. What do you want?"

Harris gave him a sad look. "So mistrustful! I just want to know where those specimens came from. They're so interesting! I'd love to talk to the person that found them, or created them or...?" He trailed off as if hoping Kaem would fill the gap."

Kaem shook his head again, "No. I promised him. Like I *told* you. It's confidential."

This time Harris's hand went into his jacket pocket. "I'd make it *very much* worth your time," he said, showing Kaem a stack of twenty-dollar bills about a half-inch thick.

Holy Methuselah! Kaem thought, *It's a good thing the person I'd be selling out would be myself. If it were someone else, I'd be really tempted.* He shook his head.

Harris added another stack of bills to make the wad of cash an inch thick.

Kaem lifted his shoulders, reluctantly saying, "Sorry."

With barely concealed anger, Harris said, "I'm *really* disappointed." He smiled, though it seemed forced. "But, if you'd at least pass on a message that I'd like to help? I'd love to be a part of whatever happens with this new... or *ancient* technology. Whatever it is, I'd love to help it reach its potential. I can see it making people's lives better and..." Harris sounded a little choked up, though Kaem thought he was putting it on, "I'd love to be a part of making the world a better place."

Extremely uncomfortable, Kaem said, "Okay, I'll pass it on." He glanced at Arya, then back to Harris, "Meanwhile, we need to get upstairs and start studying." He stepped over to the elevators and pushed the up button. Neither door opened and when he looked up, he saw the elevators were on upper floors.

Arya said, "We could take the stairs?"

Embarrassed, Kaem shook his head.

Harris stepped closer and said quietly, "What if I offered you *twice* as much as I showed you before?"

Kaem shook his head again, watching the elevator floor indicators. The one on his right was on its way down. He stepped that way, glad it took him farther from Harris.

Harris said, "What *would* it take?"

"As I said, it's confidential," Kaem said, "and *I* won't break my word." The elevator door opened and he ushered Arya in, trying to escape before he had to hear anything else Harris might say.

Once the doors closed, Arya said, "Why not take the stairs? It's only one flight."

Embarrassed, Kaem said, "My anemia's bad again. Even for one flight, I'd have to stop one or two times. And, I always have to worry that getting short of breath might make me hypoxic enough to trigger a crisis."

"Oh yeah," Arya said, sounding both embarrassed and sad. "Sorry. That was a stupid, stupid question."

"Yeah," Kaem said as the doors opened, "it was an anemist question."

Arya frowned, "Anemist?"

"Yeah," he grinned slyly, "you know, like 'sexist' but discriminatory against us anemic people."

Arya rolled her eyes. "I'm gonna be late for a… an appointment. Is there a back way out of here so I can avoid Harris if he's still down there?"

Kaem pointed, "The stairwell at the end of the hall lets out in the back."

Arya started that way.

Kaem watched her go, partly because he liked watching her, but also because he worried his flip "anemist" comment had pissed her off. Again. *She probably thinks I was making fun of her for bitching at me about sexism.* He sighed, *Maybe I was. When am I going to learn to stop making stupid jokes? She* never thinks I'm funny.

~~~

Arya felt bad about leaving Kaem in the dorm while Harris was downstairs. It seemed unlikely Harris would follow him into the private living areas so Kaem was probably safe, and she was going to be cutting it close getting to the dojo. This afternoon she was supposed to test for her shodan black belt and her sensei would *not* be amused if she were late.

Her step faltered. One of the basic tenets of her dojo was to protect those who couldn't protect themselves. *Could there be a better reason for me to be late for my test than that I needed to protect Kaem? In fact, couldn't I be criticized for rushing off to the dojo to take my test rather than fulfilling that responsibility?*

She stopped and turned around. As she started back, she saw Harris crossing the quad in front of the dorm.

He was on his way out of the area.

I guess I don't have to decide, she thought gratefully, *turning to hurry on toward the training facility.*

~~~

As Harris drove away from the campus, he thought, *Well, that's that. I gave it my best shot and... Wait...* Harris felt like little sparks of electricity were shooting back and forth in his brain. Sometimes he got great ideas when that happened.

Ah! If I hired a PI, he could follow this Kaem Seba guy around and find out who he meets with. In fact, we can call Seba and tell him we've got a hard copy of the testing results ready. We'll tell him to pick it up at the

Laurence E Dahners

lab so there's no possibility someone might skim an electronic copy off the Internet.

The PI can latch onto him when he comes out to get the results.

***

Phil Sherman parked at the bike shop across the street from Harris Laboratories. He told his phone's AI to dial James Harris. When the man picked up, Phil said, "I'm across the street. Let me know what the guy's driving when he pulls in."

Harris said, "Thank God you made it. I've been worrying you might miss him."

Patiently, Phil said, "I told you I was only ten minutes away. Besides, even if I missed him this afternoon, I'd be able to pick him up some other time. Try to relax."

"It's my party. I'll worry if I want to," Harris said truculently.

"Up to you, but I promise you, I'll pick him up and tell you *everywhere* he goes. That's what a PI does."

"I hope so. They tell me last time he was here he came in an Uber. So, whatever vehicle he comes in today, it may not be his long-term ride."

"Good to know."

Phil settled in to wait, using his rearview mirror to keep an eye on Harris Lab's parking lot. When some time had passed, he called Harris to make sure there hadn't been some screw-up with the phone call he was supposed to get.

Harris told him the kid hadn't come yet.

Phil was getting sleepy, so he opened his thermos of coffee.

92 | P a g e

It was another two hours, close to closing time for the lab, when Harris called sounding excited. "He just came in. In case you saw him in the parking lot, he's the skinny, kinda light-skinned African-American kid, probably 5'8", jeans and an orange UVA T-shirt. Arrived with a good-looking, dark-skinned girl, same height. Short, straight hair, jeans and some kind of stretchy blue top. They came in the blue Nissan parked out front."

Harris is really getting into this investigative stuff, Phil thought. He stroked his new employer's ego, "Great description. I'm on it."

~~~

When they left, Phil followed them to the UVA dorm where Harris said the kid lived. They got out and went into the dorm. The car drove away—not to the parking lot, but back to the street—suggesting it was, as advertised, an Uber.

Harris's gonna be pissed the kid didn't go right to the place they make that stuff, Phil thought, settling in to wait. He called Harris to let him know what was going on. As he'd expected, Harris was unhappy.

I'd better order a food delivery, he thought, reclining his seat and settling in to wait.

***

Up in Kaem's room, he and Arya were going over the results sheet Harris Labs had provided. To their relief, Harris himself hadn't been in evidence. They'd just picked up the envelope containing the results from Cathy, the lab's admin, and were back out the door in no time.

Laurence E Dahners

Kaem had managed to restrain himself from tearing the envelope open until they were out in the car. He'd only opened it there to be sure they had the results they'd come for. He hadn't wanted to pay to Uber back to the dorm, then find out they had the wrong data sheet.

They settled down to really study the report. Arya looked up at him, "So what do these mean? Especially the ones that say 'tested to limits.'"

"Easy ones first," Kaem said. "There, at the top, it's just giving us ordinary measurements. Telling us that, in fact, the two specimens were 7.49 x 15.01 x 1.09 mm. Not *exactly* the dimensions we thought they were, but certainly close enough. Also, not surprisingly, that their density was 1 g/cm^3, the density of the water in the stades.

"Next we've got the thermal resistance which they recorded as infinite."

"Thermal resistance?" Arya asked.

"A measure of how much heat's conducted from one side of the plate to the other. You might have heard of the 'R-value' which measures the same properties for insulation in buildings." He looked up at her, "They're saying that heat does *not* flow from one side of a stade to the other." He winked, "Lousy for your frying pans." He looked back down at the numbers, "But awesome for a lot of other uses!"

"So," Arya said thoughtfully, "you're thinking stades could be used for housing insulation?"

He looked up at her as if surprised. "Well... sure. But, more importantly, you could use them to hold hot or cold fluids."

"Ah, like the ultimate thermos. Woohoo, coffee that never gets cold?"

"*And,* liquefied gases. Liquid nitrogen, oxygen, helium. There are significant losses because heat leaks into the storage bottles, turning the liquid back to a gas that has to be released so the bottle won't overpressurize."

"Oh," Arya said thoughtfully.

"Reflectance, or the percentage of light and other radiation that bounces back was measured at 100%... They're calling the static coefficient of friction zero." Kaem snorted, "When I dropped it off, the guy told me there 'was no such thing.'"

Arya looked over his shoulder, "You're finally getting to the part where they say, 'tested to limits.'"

"Yeah, those were the tests of bending strength and heat tolerance. Apparently, the strength testing machine is limited to ten tons and their furnace only goes up to 3,000°C. The specimens didn't break and they didn't melt. So, they 'tested them to the limits' of their equipment without achieving failure."

"Ten tons sounds like a lot?"

Kaem nodded, "Especially for a plate that's only a millimeter thick. It looks like stade's stronger than graphene, which is theoretically the strongest material known."

"Is 3,000°C hot enough for a rocket engine?"

"No... But I suspect stade'll tolerate a lot more heat than that. Unfortunately, we don't have lab proven results to send to Space-Gen."

Arya chewed her lip for a moment, then said, "Maybe, once we've applied for a patent, we can send them a specimen to test for themselves." She looked over at him, "I got us an appointment with a patent lawyer tomorrow at two in the afternoon. I assume you're free?"

Laurence E Dahners

"I'm cheap," Kaem said, "not free."

Arya shook her head and got up. "I've gotta go."

~~~

As Kaem watched her leave, he thought, *Dammit! Another joke, another departure. I've got to control myself!*

***

Harris looked up when Cathy stepped into his office. "Yes?"

"Um, that young man, Kaem Seba?"

Trying to cover his jitters, Harris sat up attentively, "What?"

"When he came by to pick up the results, we forgot to give him his test specimens. Do you... Do you want me to send them by messenger or something?"

"No!" Harris said, exclaiming out of momentary dismay at the possibility. "Sorry, no. We'll keep them unless he asks for them. We don't want to waste money sending them to him when he may not want them. If he did, I'm sure he would've asked for them when he came for the results."

That's great, Harris thought after Cathy left his office. He hadn't wanted to give the specimens back, but he'd decided that it'd be worth it in order to let the PI follow the kid to wherever he took them. *Now, if only I could think of some more tests to do on the specimens.* He leaned back in his chair and closed his eyes to think. *Wait! Did Raymond test for electrical properties?* He got up and headed down the hall. Part way there, he thought, *How about corrosion resistance?*

When asked, Raymond shook his head. "Those tests weren't ticked off on the request sheet." He eyed Harris, "They aren't gonna want to pay for them."

"Yeah, but *I* want to know the results. Besides, we could justify the corrosion testing under his request that we test the specimens to destruction."

Raymond nodded, looking interested. "You want me to do the testing this morning, or wait till I finish the rest of the stuff in the queue?"

Harris said, "Do it *now*. I'm really curious about the results. I'm hoping to get the tests done before they decide to come back for their specimens."

***

Raymond set one specimen up in a salt fog corrosion chamber, then did electrical properties testing on the other one. He wasn't surprised that the mirrors not only didn't conduct electricity, but were as perfect an insulator as he'd ever encountered. They were completely nonmagnetic as well.

The next day Raymond checked on the mirror specimen he'd put in the salt fog chamber. As he'd expected, he couldn't tell the exposure to salt had done anything to the specimen. *And why would anyone think it would? Nothing fazes this stuff.* He glanced at the chemicals cabinet. *I'm gonna go right to the big guns.*

Raymond dug through their glassware and found a 10 x 20 cm glass pan. He put it in the fume hood and filled it with a few centimeters of 12 molar hydrochloric acid—as concentrated as you could get. Because he couldn't hold the slippery specimen with anything like gloves or forceps, he took a bit of time over a burner, bending a couple of glass rods into little triangles he could hook around opposing corners of the specimen. Cradling a plate with them, he slowly lowered it into the acid. He took away the glass triangles and left the plate floating on the surface of its corrosive bath. It appeared undisturbed by the acid.

Raymond turned to get a pH meter—the meter wouldn't be accurate in such a concentrated solution, but at least he could see if the pH changed with time, suggesting corrosion that might not be visible.

When he turned back, the plate had vanished. Stunned, he blinked a couple of times. He dipped a glass stirring rod in the beaker and swirled it around. The plate wasn't invisible, it was *gone*, presumably completely dissolved! *Well, we've finally found something that'll damage the stuff,* he thought. *I don't understand how it dissolved so fast though. Shouldn't it have dissolved the lower surface that was in the acid first, leaving the part that'd been floating up out of the acid behind for a bit?*

He stood and stared at the bath for a few minutes. *Maybe after it ate through the lower surface it was able to race through the rest of it?*

Raymond went to tell Harris about it.

"Really?!" Harris said.

"My sentiments exactly," Raymond said. "It isn't actually indestructible after all."

"But the salt fog test didn't hurt it, right?"

Raymond shook his head.

"Try the other specimen with a weaker acid."

"Acetic?"

"Yeah, but even with that, start with a dilute solution. Oh, and Raymond, be sure to check the pH before, during, and after this time, okay?"

"Yes, sir."

It only took a few minutes to set up the test. Once he'd recorded the pH of the solution alone at 2.38, he dipped the glass rod triangles in and swirled them around to confirm the pH didn't change. Then he used them to settle the specimen into the bath. It floated, like the other specimen had floated on the hydrochloric acid, though it didn't ride as high since acetic acid wasn't nearly as dense as HCl.

The pH was still 2.38.

Since dilute acetic acid isn't very strong, Raymond felt certain it wouldn't hurt the specimen, but when he looked up from noting his pH values this specimen had disappeared too!

The pH settled at 2.44.

It'd changed the pH, but only a little. *Could it just be dilution rather than a buffer effect?* he wondered. He tried to do some calculations and decided that diluting the acetic acid with 11.25 milliliters—the volume of the plate—of water should have raised the pH approximately that much.

Oh! He started for Harris's office. Arriving in the doorway he didn't wait to be acknowledged, instead, he just exclaimed, "It's a different state of matter!"

Harris was on the phone, but he quickly finished up and disconnected. "What?"

"Remember? Its density's 1 gram per cc, same as water? Something about putting it in acid converted it back to water from some kind of 'super-ice.'" He shrugged, "Or whatever you want to call this new state."

"Is the acetic acid doing anything?"

"Completely dissolved it. It didn't take long either."

"What?" Harris said, wide-eyed. "How dilute was it?"

"I diluted it down to the same concentration as vinegar."

"You're telling me this stuff tolerates temperatures over 3,000°C, bounces neutrons and plasma torches, takes 10 tons of bending load, but *dissolves* in vinegar?!"

Raymond nodded.

Harris sagged back in his chair, deflated. "Not exactly the kind of stuff you'd want to build with if it goes pfft on exposure to a weak acid."

Raymond said, "I don't know. For material properties like that it'd probably be worth dipping it in plastic or something else that completely seals it away from the environment. Hell, you're probably going to have to cover it anyway, just to keep everything from slipping off of it."

"There go my frictionless railroad skids though."

"Yeah, but the kinds of things you could build out of it if you just protected it from acid… I mean, *Holy Shit!*"

Harris nodded thoughtfully, "There is that."

Raymond said, "The industries built on this are going to be worth billions! Trillions! Have you figured out who's making it yet? I've gotta buy some stock!"

Shit! Harris thought, worried about loose lips giving away his game. *Though how I could've thought Raymond wouldn't figure this out is beyond me. The guy's not stupid.* To Raymond, he said, "No, I have no idea. They didn't write it on the forms." He didn't say anything about his other efforts to determine the source, but had a feeling that Raymond somehow suspected them. He gave the man a serious look, "You shouldn't joke about buying stock. Remember, the test results are supposed to be confidential. Buying stock would be insider trading."

Raymond gave him an odd look for a moment, then said, "Absolutely right boss, I wouldn't even dream of it." After a moment's hesitation, he followed up with, "I was just joking with you. I wouldn't joke about that with anyone else."

For a moment Harris thought Raymond was going to wink at him, but he didn't. Harris said, "The question's whether we owe them a report about the fact that we finally found a way to test their plates to destruction?"

Raymond shook his head, "They didn't *ask* for electrical properties, corrosion testing, or chemical resistance."

They did ask us to test to destruction though, Harris thought. After a moment, he said, "Agreed. We won't tell them unless they ask. But we've got to realize that they may want their specimens back. If they ask for them, we'll have to tell them they were destroyed by low pH."

Raymond nodded, "Sure... If."

Chapter Seven

Contacting Space-Gen

As Kaem got in the Uber, Arya said, "I realized we left those two stade specimens out at Harris Laboratories. I was thinking, after we finish talking to the patent attorney, we should swing by and pick them up. Save the cost of a third Uber to go get them some other time."

Kaem gave her a little smile. "I think that'd be a waste of time."

"You want to let Harris keep the specimens? What if he figures something out from them?"

Kaem said, "I really don't think there's anything to *be* figured out from them. It's not like there's any kind of analysis that'll let him discover what they are. Pretty much everything he does just bounces off. In fact, I was thinking there wouldn't be any great harm in sending some specimens to companies like Space-Gen. They can do testing and see that stade's essentially the perfect material for a rocket, but there's no way for them to figure out what it is or make it themselves." He shrugged, "In fact, I think it'd be so impossible to reverse engineer, that we just don't have to worry much about a patent. All we need to do is keep our 'formula' for making stade a secret."

"I don't know," Arya said unhappily. "What if someone decides the only way to get the formula's to beat it out of us?"

"If they're that evil, why not wait till we make millions, then steal the *money*?"

She shrugged, "But they're good at making rockets. They don't have the skills it takes to steal money."

"I don't think people that're good at making rockets are the kind of people who'd try to beat the formula out of us." He hesitated, "Out of me, actually, since you don't know how it's made."

"But, *they* don't know that. I think I'd be in for a beating too."

"Oh, yeah. Sorry. I hadn't considered that possibility."

"Why're you in such a hurry? We just get our patent, *then* we start selling it."

"I..." he trailed off.

"'You,' what?"

Wistfully, he said, "I'm *so* tired of being sick all the time. Weak, short of breath, unable to do... do *anything!* I want gene therapy *now*, not 'someday.'"

"Sorry," Arya said, eyes full of sympathy. "You're right." She sighed, "How about this? I've read that if you don't have the money for a patent, one option is to show a company your idea under what's called a 'nondisclosure agreement.' Essentially, they sign a binding contract saying they won't steal your idea before they get to see the technology, then if they want the tech, *they* pay for the patent. The patent's still in your name. You just agree to license the technology to them."

"That sounds great!" Kaem said enthusiastically, "Let's ask the attorney about that."

"I don't know about that. He'll have a conflict of interest because he'd like to be the one who files for the patent."

Laurence E Dahners

Kaem shrugged, "Even if Space-Gen insists on using their own patent attorneys, I'd think we'd want to have our guy look over the application to protect our interests."

Arya said, "Maybe we can sell him on that." They rode for a few moments in silence, then she said, "I still think we should pick those specimens up from Harris Labs."

"There's nothing to pick up."

Arya frowned, "You already got them?"

"No, they were set for one megasecond or 11.6 days. The one with the cricket expired this morning. The cricket looks healthy by the way. The test samples were made on the same afternoon, just a little while later than the one with the cricket, using the same settings on the machine. Therefore, stasis on the test samples would've expired this morning as well. If we tried to pick them up all we'd get would be a couple of wet envelopes."

"Oh," Arya said thoughtfully. She giggled. "I'd like to say that I hope they didn't get something else wet and ruin it, but I don't like that Harris guy."

"Me either," Kaem said with a little grin.

~~~

The patent attorney reluctantly agreed to draft nondisclosure agreements for them to send to companies.

They never showed him the sample stade they'd had with them.

***

On edge, Harris met the PI, Phil Sherman, at a coffee shop. "What can I get you?" he asked when Sherman sat down.

Once they had their coffees, Harris leaned across the table of their back corner booth and asked, "What can you tell me?"

Sherman held up a finger, "One bizarre thing. I don't know if it matters, but he never goes anywhere without that girl."

"Really? I'm pretty sure she wasn't with him the day he dropped off the specimen."

Sherman shrugged, then snickered, "Maybe they just started dating. They could be in the *hot throes of love*."

Feeling certain the girl didn't matter, Harris impatiently asked, "Where've they been?"

"To the physics building, where I assume his classes are." He cocked his head, "The hot girlfriend actually came by his dorm, they walked to the physics building together, then she went on to the business school. It's like he's blind or helpless or something and needs to have her guide him." He snorted, "She came back in the middle of the day and they sat outside and ate lunches they'd packed. They're discreet though. I didn't even see any kissing. Then they snagged an Uber."

Harris had been uninterested, but the Uber piqued his interest. Anxiously he asked, "I hope you were able to follow them?"

"Of course," Sherman said, sounding a little offended, "It's *what I do*. They went to see Thomas Morales, a patent attorney. Spent an hour and fifteen minutes inside, then took another Uber back to his dorm."

A patent attorney! Did that kid invent the technology himself?! It seemed impossible. Feeling frenzied, but trying to hide his tension, Harris asked, "I don't suppose there's any way to know what they talked about?"

"Not without doing something illegal."

"Oh," Harris said disappointedly.

He was wondering if there were any other angles when Sherman slid a handwritten note across the table, keeping his fingers on it. The words were at odd angles. It said, "illegal," at one angle and "premium $," at another.

Harris looked a question at Sherman.

Sherman pulled his note back and wrote "5X" on it at a third angle.

Five times as much! Harris thought with alarm. He'd already thought Sherman's prices were exorbitant. *But,* he reminded himself, *I'm never gonna get a chance like this again.*

Harris raised his eyes to Sherman's, then gave a slow deliberate nod. He gestured for the pencil.

Sherman turned the paper to a different angle, then handed Harris the pencil while not letting go of the paper.

Harris wrote, "need know," and in another spot, "what's in patent."

Sherman pulled the paper back. At one angle, he wrote "$20,000." At another angle, he wrote, "If successful."

Harris wondered why the guy kept changing the angle and writing on different parts of the paper. Then, as he studied the confusing mess the writing had made, he realized that it made it impossible to tell what order things had been written in. And, thus hard to piece the conversation together. He raised his eyes to Sherman's and nodded again.

Sherman turned the paper and wrote, "need Seba," and, "email addr"

Sherman asked, "Anything else?

Harris shook his head.

Sherman slowly and deliberately tore the piece of paper into little bits, dropped them in the last of his coffee, then drank it down. He reached across the table and shook Harris's hand, then got up and started for the coffee shop's door.

Am I going over the edge again? Harris wondered, acutely aware of how many doses of his meds he'd skipped in an effort to boost his mental acuity during this critical time. He started to call Sherman back, then shook his head. *I'll never get an opportunity like this again. Besides,* he thought angrily, justifying himself, *a snot-nosed kid like that doesn't* deserve *to keep something this important to himself.*

***

Arya and Kaem worked together to email and snail-mail letters to the chief technical officers of every space launch company for which they could get addresses.

And all the space launch wannabes.

Out of respect for the recently adopted country of both of their families, they limited the mailings to American companies for now.

The letters enthusiastically described the benefits of using stade as a material for building rockets.

They attached copies of the Harris Laboratories documentation of the properties of a stade and the nondisclosure agreement or NDA to the letter.

***

Harris and Sherman met at a different coffee shop. Trying not to exhibit the tension crackling through him, Harris said, "What's up?"

Sherman slowly shook his head. "computer's impenetrable."

Not sure of the meaning of Sherman's cryptic words, this time Harris pulled out his own piece of paper. He wrote, "Seba's?"

Sherman nodded.

Harris wrote, "hire a better hacker!"

Sherman pulled out his own piece of paper. He wrote, "using the best I can find."

"going through trash?"

"housekeeper says all shredded."

Harris rubbed his temples in frustration. He asked, "Are you giving up?"

"No. I still have some ideas." He wrote, "says Seba's computer," and "security incredible." At another angle, he wrote, "REALLY smart." Sherman tapped that last statement with a finger, then Seba's name. He said, "Something you should take into consideration."

***

Mary Willis, Senior assistant to Mahesh Prakant, Space-Gen's Chief Technical Officer, studied the letter her assistant brought her. It was an unsolicited request that Space-Gen sign a nondisclosure agreement to look at a new material. The writers promised their material would be useful for building rockets.

Generally, her boss was interested in new technology, but this didn't seem to be coming from any known space technology company. In fact, reading the letter, she'd swear it came from a small group of individuals. A phone number was the only contact information. She thought the likelihood it was someone's pipe dream must be high. With some trepidation, she decided to forward it to her boss. He always claimed he wanted to see *all* the new technology offered to Space-Gen. Unfortunately, sometimes he blew up when he decided the technology was a waste of his time. After a little thought, she applied a Post-it note apologizing for wasting his time if he wasn't interested.

~~~

The next day, Prakant dropped the letter and NDA on her desk. "Why'd you forward *this* to me?!"

Biting her tongue, Willis said, "You told me you wanted to see *all* proposals for new technology."

"But did you even look at the material properties they're claiming?!"

She shook her head, "I don't know much about—"

"They're impossible! I can't believe I wasted my time reading the letter before noticing the *ridiculous* claims they're making for material data!"

"Sorry. Shouldn't I forward these queries in the future?"

"No," Prakant sighed, "and I'm sorry. I shouldn't expect you to know what's possible and what's not. In the future though, before you forward things like this to me, have one of the junior engineers look at them and decide if they're even plausible."

He turned abruptly and walked away before she could acknowledge his instructions.

***

It'd been a couple of weeks. As they walked to class, Arya said, "We've gotten replies from most of the space launch companies we sent NDAs."

Sure the answer would be disheartening, Kaem kept his tone upbeat nonetheless, "Any takers?"

"No. Most of the replies have been versions of, 'Not interested.' The ones who've given a reason for the rejection have said something about the claimed properties being ridiculous or impossible. Many of them have a kind of boilerplate statement about how they don't want to look at technology that might conflict with something they already have in the pipeline. I get the impression the legal issue is that if we showed them something they're already working on, that when they put it into practice, we might claim they stole the idea from us."

"They aren't working on 'something like this'!"

"You're preaching to the choir." She sighed, "The frequency of the replies has dropped off. I think the remaining companies probably tossed our letters in the trash."

"We're going to have to send them samples."

"Mr. Morales strongly advised against that."

"He knows the law, but he doesn't have any idea how hard it'd be to reverse engineer stade."

"Okay," Arya said reluctantly, "I'll look at our mailing list, then call Gunnar and ask him to make us enough test stades to send one to every company."

"Two for every company," Kaem said. "But, remember, he can't make them without the electronics. We'll have to go over there and help him make them."

"Okay, I'll work out a time we can go over." She frowned, "I keep forgetting to bring this up, but I'm worried about you keeping that rack of electronics in your room. You've told me about that fancy encryption you're using on your computer, and I know you shred every bit of paper, but what if someone just stole the electronics. Aren't they the most important part of the whole thing?"

"Yeah," Kaem said, "Gunnar couldn't make stades with just the mirrored cavities, he'd need the electronics. The electronics can't make stade without his cavities, which is why I keep them separated. It just makes it harder for someone to copy the whole thing."

"Supposing someone's been following us around and they know about Gunnar. If they took a cavity from him and stole the electronics from your room…"

"I change every setting on that rack of electronics when we're not using it. You've probably noticed I even unplug the wires that go from one component to the next. There's a ginormous number of possible settings and another vast number of ways they could be wired up. Very few of them would actually work—"

"Okay, okay," Arya said putting her hands up in surrender. "I'm trusting you on this one…" she hesitated a moment. "I've got a request. I know we're not going to make any new molds, so I can't have my perfectly insulated coffee cup. But is there a way we could leave little holes around the edges of the 7.5 x 15 cm test samples this time? I'd like to make extra plates and use them to line my coat. Use that perfect insulator to turn my lightweight jacket into something that's warm enough for the depths of winter."

Kaem frowned, "We could make holes if Gunnar could silver the circumference of little pieces of glass rod and stick them into the mold so they'd bridge from the top to the bottom." He gave her a puzzled look,

"Then you're what? Going to sew the plates into your jacket using the holes to send your threads through?"

Arya shrugged, "I'll see when I've got them. I've been thinking I could use fine cord to bind them together into a kind of vest. Then I'd sew that vest into my jacket between the liner and the shell." She gave him a curious look, "Wouldn't the holes make them easier to handle too? They wouldn't get away from people all the time because you could loop a string through the holes to serve as kind of a handle."

"Maybe. Go ahead and call Gunnar. See if he can set up the molds to make the holes without it costing an arm and a leg."

***

Harris was studying a photograph Sherman had provided. Apparently, it'd been taken in Kaem Seba's dorm by one of the housekeeping people. It showed a rack of electronics. Harris could see the settings on each of the components in the rack. However, all the connecting wires had been unjacked so he didn't know how one component hooked to the next. He sighed. *Even if I knew how to hook them all together, and the settings turned out to be correct, I don't even know if this equipment has anything to do with making the wonder-material. And even if I got all the electronics and they* do *have something to do with making that stuff, I don't know what I'd hook the wires up to since I don't think just wiring them correctly and powering them up is suddenly going to make that... substance appear out of thin air.*

He'd priced and considered ordering all the electronic gear "just in case" but decided it was ridiculous to spend that much money on equipment until he had *some* idea what he would do with it.

***

While Kaem was setting up his rack of electronics, Gunnar hooked the cables up to the lasers and microwave antennas. Then he carefully poured water into the 7.5 x 15 cm x 1 mm chamber. Gunnar had argued for making a few other shapes to send the companies for testing, but Kaem thought it'd be a waste of money. He claimed if they didn't understand how important stade could be to rocketry from the current samples, they'd never figure it out. It hadn't been hard to put in little silvered glass posts that should leave holes around the edges of the plates, so at least they had some variety.

Gunnar carefully closed the door over the water, squeezing out the excess. Kaem looked ready, so Gunnar gave him a nod. Kaem flipped a switch and heard the charging whine and snap of the big capacitor. Gunnar opened the door and popped out the stade. Since he was ready for it, he managed to grab it with hands on both sides before it slid off the bench. He stepped over to Arya who was holding open a 5 x 7 envelope. He dropped the stade in and Arya sealed it up.

Kaem said, "Wait a minute," and stepped over to heft the envelope. "Why's it so heavy?"

"It's not heavy," Gunnar said, puzzled.

"Oh, wait," Kaem said as if he'd had a realization. "You made it out of water, didn't you?"

"Yes," Gunnar said patiently. "You said we were making more like the last ones."

"I did, didn't I?" Kaem said as if amused at himself. "One small detail. Rocketry's all about weight. We should send *them* ones that're air-filled so they're light."

"We could make them with helium..." Gunnar said eagerly, looking at the chamber and wondering how much helium he could get to stay in its shallow cavity.

"I think that's just a little too far out there," Kaem said with a laugh. "We can sell them on that idea *after* they buy air-filled ones."

"But with helium, the engines would actually be lighter than air!"

"And," Kaem said with a snort, "the samples would be really hard to test. I'm picturing them trying to get them down off the ceiling and into their three-point testing jig. All the while, the sample's slipping out of their hands and shooting back up to the ceiling again and again."

Gunnar grinned, "They're," he made finger quotes, "'*rocket scientists*!' They should be smart enough to tie a string through one of our new holes."

Kaem laughed. "I think *some* rocket scientists are pretty obtuse."

Gunnar wiped out the chamber with a paper towel and they started making the test samples.

Plus, a bunch more so Arya could line her super-jacket.

~~~

In his car on the street across from Gunnar Schmidt's backyard workshop, Phil Sherman listened to the audio stream coming in through the laser microphone he'd focused on the shop's window. *I don't think any of this stuff's going to be of any use to Harris,* he thought. *None of it makes any sense.*

***

Oh, my, God! Harris thought as he listened to the recording of Seba and this Gunnar Schmidt out in Schmidt's workshop. *Rocket engines! Of course! Raymond was right, the stuff would be amazing for construction, but the BIG money's going to be in rocket engines. Extreme pressures, extreme temperatures, extreme costs of failure.* He knew Raymond hadn't been able to test the material up to the kind of temperatures found in a rocket engine, but he felt sure the stuff would tolerate temperatures *far* higher than Raymond had subjected it to.

He had another thought, *Sounds like Raymond was right about the stuff being another state of matter. Raymond guessed it was another form of water and now Seba says it was made out of water. But what the hell's this stuff about making them out of "air?"* Harris could understand that it'd be nice to have an exotic material that was light as air, but he couldn't fathom how you could change the state of matter of "air" since it was a mixture of several different gases. If you tried to change the state of air to "frozen," first the water vapor froze, then the carbon dioxide, the argon, the nitrogen, and finally the oxygen. You'd have layers of different materials of different densities rather than an apparently homogenously dense material like the mirrored plates.

Maybe if they start with air. They let water, carbon dioxide, and argon condense out, then make their material out of the nitrogen when it condenses? Maybe, but how the hell do they get to this new state?!

He closed his eyes in frustration. *However they do it, I've got to get on board with them,* he thought. *But how?*

Chapter Eight

A specimen of Stade

Mary looked up when she heard her assistant let out a little grunt. The young man was batting something around his cubicle. It was flashy. Her first thought was that he'd folded up a piece of aluminum foil and started playing some kind of game—the kind of silly juggling game that gave some young men such pleasure.

She blinked. Whatever he was knocking around looked like a mirror. And it seemed to float through the air without falling. She wondered, *Mylar balloon, almost depleted of its helium?* Gabe finally got it with a solid grab and Mary thought the fun was over... but the damned thing got away from him.

Mary stood and cleared her throat. She didn't want Mr. Prakant coming in and, not only finding Gabe playing some kind of juvenile game, but also finding Mary sitting there watching him like a spectator.

Gabe gave her a sheepish glance, then said, "Sorry Ms. Willis." He made another grab, but the thing got away from him again. She had the feeling it would've flown across the room except that it flew something like a feather does—slowly, with floaty twisting.

It was coming her way, so in order to put a stop to the foolishness, she stepped over and caught it. Cleanly, she thought. After all, she'd been a three-sport athlete in high school. But when her fingers closed on it, it simply slipped through them. *Like trying to catch a greased piglet, but worse,* she thought, remembering the trick her brothers had played on her back when they were kids on the farm.

She wiped her fingers, expecting oil, but they seemed clean. Remembering how they'd caught the pig, she stepped after it and surrounded it with a basket of her fingers. *Success!*

She turned on the shamefaced Gabe, "What *is* this!" Partly she was asking a rhetorical question about how he'd come to be screwing around, and partly she wanted to know where she could get a slippery, floats-in-air mirror for her grandkids.

"Um, it came in the mail, Ms. Willis."

Mary blinked. "In the mail?"

He nodded. "It's like the letter we got before, but this time it came in a 9 x 12 envelope with smaller envelopes inside. One of the smaller envelopes had this mirror in it."

"Let me see."

He took her to his desk and showed her the envelope and the smaller 5 x 7 envelope that'd had the mirror in it. She had him hold it open so she could slide the mirror back in it.

She riffled through the papers. One was an NDA and she thought it was the same as the document she'd given Prakant before. The letter was different though. Of note, it said, "...we have become concerned that interest in our new material, Stade, has been low because the various companies we've offered options on the material have not believed its physical properties are possible. Therefore, we are providing these test samples so you can evaluate the suitability of the material yourself. We would note that the material's low weight, heat tolerance, and extreme strength make it especially suitable for rocket engines and its extreme thermal resistance makes it particularly good for cryogenic tankage…"

Mary contemplated how to proceed and felt a knot forming in her stomach. Should she give this to a junior engineer like Prakant had told her, or did his previous rejection still stand? Then she thought about the floating mirror. *That stuff's so… unbelievable. Could it actually be something new?*

~~~

Mary walked into one of the big open-plan spaces where many of the junior engineers worked. She wasn't sure who to talk to, so she stood fidgeting for a moment. A pleasant-looking young man, stopped on his way by, "Can I help you?"

"Yes, thank you," she said, then pulled out her big gun, "I'm Mr. Prakant's assistant. He told me to have a junior engineer evaluate a new material. Whom would you suggest?"

When she looked up at him, she got the impression he'd just finished rolling his eyes. Pointing at a young woman working in front of a large display covered with design drawings, he said, "Take it to April Lee, she's the most junior." He chuckled, "They always get saddled with the crap jobs."

As Mary walked over, she wondered whether Lee was really the most junior, or just the most junior woman. Should Mary be upset that she'd been told to dump a crap job on a woman, or excited that a woman might get an amazing opportunity with this weird material? She stopped just behind Lee's shoulder and waited to be noticed.

Lee seemed very focused and didn't notice Mary's presence. After a minute passed, Mary cleared her throat.

Lee turned, looking harried. "Yes?" she asked impatiently.

Feeling terrible, Mary said, "Hi. We've received a sample of a new material from an outside vendor. Mr. Prakant's asked to have it evaluated."

Lee frowned. "Why are you bringing it to me? I'm very junior."

Uncomfortably, Mary said, "Um, Mr. Prakant told me to have it evaluated by a junior engineer before—"

Lee interrupted, her eyes darting around the room, "Who put you up to this?"

"Um, Mr. Prakant said—"

"Who are you?"

Mary stiffened a little, irritated at being treated so abruptly by the young woman. Drawing herself up, "I'm Mary Willis, Mr. Prakant's assistant."

"And he told you to bring this to *me*? He doesn't even know who I am."

"No. He said to take it to a junior engineer and see if it was worth wasting his time on. So—"

"And how'd you come to pick *me*?"

"A young man told me you were the most junior," Mary said, turning to look for the young man who'd said it. To her dismay she saw a number of young men looking her way and grinning. The one who'd told her to bring it to Lee looked hugely amused.

Lee said, "It was Jerome Stitt, wasn't it? That blond prick over there with the shit-eating grin on his face?"

Mary looked. Lee was pointing at the guy. "Yes," she said restraining her anger until she could be sure it was warranted. "Are you *not* the most junior?"

"No! I'm just the one those immature assholes like to crap on."

Mary's temper flared, but she tamped it down. Stepping closer to Lee, she leaned down and spoke in a low voice, "I'd like to suggest that you take a quick look at this material. It really is astonishing. Perhaps the best revenge you could have on those guys would come from being the one to bring it to Prakant's attention?"

"Yeah, like *I'd* ever be the one who got to show it to him."

"*I* can make that happen," Mary said.

Lee gave her an appraising look. "Really?"

Mary returned a decisive nod. "Look at the sample. If you don't think it's interesting, tell me which junior engineer to take it to."

Looking reluctant, Lee said, "I'd have to take it down for a lot of testing before I'd know anything. And, I've got assigned work stacking up."

Frustrated, Mary said, "Let's just walk over to that side conference room and get out the specimen for you to see and touch. I promise you; you've never seen anything like it. If you don't think it's worth more testing, I'll abjectly apologize."

Lee held out her hand, "All right, all right! I'll look at it, but I don't need to go to a conf—"

This time Mary interrupted Lee. "If I show it to you here, all those idiots," she gestured back behind her, "are going to see it and it won't be just *your* discovery."

"Just put it here, on my desk," Lee said, rolling her eyes. "They won't see it; we'll be blocking their line of sight."

"Trust me for a moment—"

"Just *show* it to me!"

Mary exploded, though quietly. "Do you think I'm *stupid*?" she hissed. Lee looked up with a flash of anger, but Mary interrupted her before Lee could even begin to speak. Mary continued, "I'm *trying* to help you by giving you an opportunity to evaluate something unique and take it to the boss. *You're* being a bitch! Now, either you do it my way or I'll go find some other young engineer and give this opportunity to her!"

Lee took a big breath and let it out slowly. She stiffly got up from her chair and turned toward the conference rooms. Mary heard her mutter, "This better be good."

Mary closed the door behind them after they entered. Opening the big envelope, she got out the papers and the two small envelopes.

Lee pounced on the papers as soon as she saw the top one was titled "Material Properties."

Mary was opening one of the smaller envelopes when Lee disgustedly said, "Oh, this is absolute *bullshit!*"

Mary froze with an anxious feeling that she'd misread the uniqueness of what they'd been sent. Then she remembered how hard it was to catch the mirrors. Grinning to herself, she pulled the smaller envelope open and held it out to Lee. "Here's a sample."

Lee stood, "I don't need to see it. Hell, they didn't even print up honest material property results…"

She'd turned to go when Mary pinched the sample at its back end and it shot out of the envelope in front of Lee. As before, it flew like a weightless feather, tumbling slower and slower through the air, but not falling. Startled, Lee drew back, eyes widening in astonishment, "What the hell!"

Mary said, "It's really light, *isn't* it?"

"*This* is their sample?!" Lee said, watching the slowly twisting mirror.

Mary nodded, waiting impatiently for Lee to try to grab it, anticipating the amusement of watching her fail.

"Wait," Lee said, turning back to the material data sheet. "I thought they claimed a density of 1g/cc? That thing shouldn't float... Oh, someone penciled in that *our* samples are lighter. They can't have the same specs then!" She turned to look at the floating mirror, musing to herself, "What is it, some kind of aerogel?" She looked down at the specs, then turned back to the mirror, "But an aerogel couldn't even *approach* these other properties..."

Finally, Lee reached for the mirror. Mary choked back a snort when the mirror slid right through her fingers.

Lee looked at her fingers, probably searching for oil like Mary had when she'd first encountered the material. Lee wiped her fingers on her pants, then reached for the mirror again. This time when the mirror slipped away, Mary couldn't hold in her giggle.

Lee gave her a look, "You *knew* it was this slippery?"

"Oh, yes," Mary said, a little breathlessly. "It got out of the envelope over in my office. Had a hell of a time getting it back in."

"And you didn't say anything because...?"

"You wouldn't have believed me anyway. Besides, it *says* the coefficient of friction's zero right there on the material properties sheet."

"But... that's *ridiculous*..." Lee said. This time she spoke plaintively rather than angrily. She made another couple of attempts to capture the sample.

Mary stepped over and caught it in a basket of her fingers, then presented it to Lee. "Here, feel it while I've got it trapped."

Gingerly Lee did so. "It's warm," she said with surprise.

Mary nodded, "And it really does seem frictionless, doesn't it?"

Lee slowly shook her head. "That's not..." she broke off, sliding her fingers back and forth over the specimen. "Sure feels that way though," she said, as if talking to herself. She looked up at Mary, "Can you hold it still while I try to bend it?"

Mary nodded and Lee reached between Mary's fingers to grasp the plate and try to bend it like you might fold a piece of paper.

Lee drew her head back, seeming surprised. "It *can't* be that strong, can it?" she asked, as if to herself.

Mary nodded, "Don't the specs say it's really strong?"

Lee shrugged, "Yeah, but they're claiming strength that's beyond the realm of plausible. There's no material even close to what they're contending."

"Their letter says this's something completely new..."

Lee let go of the sample and pulled out a chair. "Let me read what they've said." She picked up the sheaf of papers from the envelope and started reading the letter. "They don't even give an address!" she exclaimed. She shook her head disbelievingly, "As if this is from a *person*, not a company!"

Mary, said, "There's a twist tie on the papers there. Can you put it through one of the holes to provide a grip? Then open the envelope so I can slide this back in it? I've got work to do and I trust you're able to decide whether or not this is worth Mr. Prakant's time without me?"

"Yes," Lee said, popping to her feet. "Thanks for bringing this to me… and especially for keeping after me until I actually gave it a look. I… I apologize for the way I acted."

Mary started to say it was okay, but stopped. Instead, she gave Lee a little grin, "You *should* apologize. You were acting like a *man*. I was just about to find someone nice to give it to."

"Sorry," Lee said, looking abashed. "I'd like to make the defense that the guys in that room have driven me crazy, but… really, there *isn't* any excuse."

"Right," Mary said, giving her a wink, "there isn't. But we girls need to stick together, so, if you decide it's worth Mr. Prakant's time, call me. Mary Willis. I'll get you an appointment and help you get your revenge on the boys."

***

James Harris looked in the mirror. He thought, *I look like shit warmed over.*

He hadn't been sleeping. Just lying awake at night suffering from FOMO—fear of missing out—in the worst way. *That little shit's going to change the world and I'm not going to be part of it. He's gonna be richer than Midas and I won't have a scrap of that either.*

He took a Tums and reminded himself he wasn't about to *lose* money; he was only going to miss out on getting rich. *It's not a disaster, only a missed opportunity.*

Shaking his head at his own seemingly uncontrollable impulses, he went to his closet and got out his 9mm. He disassembled and cleaned it. He checked his ammunition. It was five years old. He realized he had no idea how long ammo lasted. *I'd better get a new box,* he thought distantly.

He wandered out into the family room. His wife studied him for a moment. "Jim…? You're taking your meds, right?"

"Uh-huh," he lied. He didn't feel guilty about it. His meds dulled the sharpness he'd need to handle this situation.

***

Mary ushered April Lee into Mr. Prakant's office. "Mr. Prakant, this is April Lee, the young engineer I told you about. She's the one who took on the testing of that new material you told me to have evaluated." Feeling like she was babbling, Mary shut up.

"Hello, Ms. Lee. What'd you find?" Prakant laughed, "Mary's sure excited about it. I know the properties of their material can't be what they claimed, but if they're even a little better than what we've got…?"

Lee didn't seem intimidated talking to the CTO, but Mary thought that might be because of what she'd learned in the testing lab. Lee said, "Sir, the stuff may be even more astonishing than the numbers they sent you the first time." She bulled ahead despite Prakant's raised eyebrows. "The density they reported was 1g/cc, the same as water, but the sample we received has a density of 0.00122 g/cc, about the same as air, depending on temperature and pressure."

"What?! And they're solid?"

Lee nodded.

"You realize they'd float in the air if that were so?"

"Of course, sir." She held the 5 x 7 envelope out vertically and unfolded its flap.

Prakant reached out for it, but Lee jerked the envelope down quickly, leaving the 3 x 6-inch mirror floating in the air before Prakant. Prakant blinked at it for a moment, then reached out, saying, "You think it's partially filled with helium?"

Lee didn't address the question, instead saying, "It really is frictionless, sir..." she broke off when Prakant grabbed at the mirror and it promptly slipped out of his grasp.

"What the hell?" Prakant said, looking first at his fingertips, then back at the mirror. "What in all damnation?!" He grabbed at it again. It got away from him a second time.

Proving she'd learned from Mary, Lee stepped over and surrounded it with a basket of fingers. "It's the perfect bearing material, sir. Completely frictionless."

Prakant gave her a stunned look, "But it can't be *strong* enough for a bearing. Helium filled; it'd have incredibly thin walls." He shook his head, "No matter what the walls are made of, it has to be weak..." he trailed off thoughtfully, tilting his head as he studied it. "Maybe it's an aerogel using helium? A heliogel, so to speak?"

Lee quietly said, "Sir, it's so strong we can't reach its limits with our testing equipment."

Prakant's eyes flashed up to Lee's, then back to the specimen. "You're saying..." He trailed off uncertainly.

"Sir, we built a fixture for this very specimen and loaded it in three-point bending to 14 metric tons-force, which is when the bearing surface of the fixture sheared off. As you can see, the specimen was undamaged." Lee paused at the confused look on Prakant's face, then spoke as if she were comforting him, "I know it looks like it *must* be weak. You can stress it with your fingers while I've got it immobilized if you'd like?"

Prakant stepped closer and reached between Lee's fingers to try to bend the mirror. He grunted, blanching his fingers with the pressure, then let go, shaking his head in disbelief. He leaned down to study it more closely. "There aren't even any fingerprints on it!"

"No, sir. *Nothing* sticks to it."

Prakant blinked. "What're you thinking we could use it for?"

"Sir, it's a perfect insulator. If you made a tank out of it and filled it with liquid hydrogen, it'd stay liquid without any active cooling. *Indefinitely*, sir."

With a small shake of his head, Prakant said, "Well, there'd be *some* losses..."

He trailed off as Lee shook her head. "There wouldn't be if the tank and its cap were entirely made of stade. Its thermal resistance seems as close to infinite as it can be."

"Stade?"

"That's what they call their material." She waited a beat for Prakant to comment, when he didn't, she continued, "And, it's incredibly heat tolerant. We've been unable to heat it to its limits. Hell, we can't even heat it enough to turn it black. We clamped this one I'm holding inside the combustion chamber of one of the test engines. After a firing, it looked exactly like it does now—like a perfect, unsmudged mirror. Essentially, it's *the* perfect material for a rocket engine. We wouldn't have to cryocool the walls to keep them from melting and, even if the walls of the combustion chamber were only a millimeter thick, like this test sample, the propellant couldn't generate enough pressure to blow it out." She snorted, "Though there's no need to make it with thin walls. After all, an engine and tanks made of this stuff wouldn't mass any more than if they were made of air!"

Prakant abruptly sat down and picked up the sheet with the results of Lee's material testing. After perusing the results for a minute, he asked, "How much do they want for this stuff?" His eyes went back to the sample. "And how are we supposed to machine it into an engine?"

Looking as if she felt uncomfortable looming over her boss, Lee sat down too. "Sir, I called the phone number they gave for technical questions. I had to leave a message. The guy who called me back said if we'd provide them with a glass mold suitable for pouring the components, they'd pour us an engine."

Prakant stared at her for a moment. "Pour?" He looked down at the sample Lee still held in her basketed fingers. "It starts as a liquid?"

"Well, he said it isn't really a liquid, but that we could think of it that way."

"And how much does the stuff cost?"

"He read somewhere that each engine costs us two-million dollars. He said they'd make engines to our design out of stade for that price." Lee gave him an inquisitive look, "How much *do* our engines cost us?"

Prakant waggled his hand, "A little more than that. But that includes a lot of plumbing that they're probably not planning to manufacture for us."

Lee gave him a curious look, "Wouldn't a lot of that plumbing be unneeded if the material for the engine didn't have to be cooled by pumping cryo fuel through it?"

Prakant gave a thoughtful nod. "A lot of it wouldn't. A glass mold?"

"Yes, sir. It has to be transparent to light."

"How do we get the glass out of the combustion chamber after it's formed? A combustion chamber can't be made in pieces we can disassemble to take the glass out of the mold."

"I asked him that. He said we had two choices. One, we could break or melt the glass that filled the chamber—"

"But…!" Prakant interrupted, then he paused thoughtfully. "Sorry, I keep forgetting this material's practically indestructible. Of course, we can break or melt the glass out of it."

Lee nodded. "I had the same reaction. The other possibility is that, using stade, we actually *could* make a two-part chamber that screwed or bolted together. Um," Lee hesitated, "the technical guy pointed out that threads in stade have to be coarse because so far they can't form features under 1mm. Also, because stade's frictionless and non-deformable, anything that's threaded together will just come unscrewed. You literally *won't be able* to screw it tight. We'll have to work out a system for holding bolts tightly screwed."

Looking dazed, Prakant said, "Ask them if they can make us some samples that aren't just flat plates."

"Already did. He said if we can make a glass mold, they'll fill it with stade. But they won't give us any more free samples. They're going to charge us like it's made of gold."

Prakant snorted, "That'll be cheap, the stuff's practically weightless."

"Priced like gold by volume, not weight."

"Damn!" Prakant said, though Mary didn't think he was really angry. He leaned back in his chair and laced his hands behind his head. After staring into space for a moment, he sat back up and looked at Lee. "Great job and an amazing find Ms...." He trailed off, "Sorry, I knew your name when you came in here, but I've become rather discombobulated..."

"Lee, sir. April Lee, but I prefer to go by Lee. Thank you."

"Okay, I'm not taking this away from you, but you've got to move it along. Get help from whoever you need to. Demand it. Tell me if anyone stonewalls you. I want you to call these people and tell them we're interested. Ask them if we can get exclusive rights to the material. Figure out what constraints there are on making molds. Talk to the people in prototyping and tell them we need to form a glass mold for a small engine and a LOX tank. Big enough to work burning liquid hydrogen and oxygen but small enough not to break the bank at the price of gold, eh? That means you need to engineer it to use as little stade as possible. Anytime someone gives you trouble, use my name. Liberally. If they resist, call me."

He gave her a hard look, "I want this to happen and I want it to happen NOW. We do *not* want one of our competitors to beat us to this, understand?"

Lee looked like she'd gained an inch. "Yes, sir!"

Prakant waved her away, "Go, go, go, go!"

Lee turned and left the room. As she passed Mary she mouthed, "Thank you!"

Mary followed her out. As she left, she heard Prakant phoning his second-in-command, telling him to provide Lee all available support.

Mary smiled. It felt good.

Chapter Nine

Harris "negotiates"

Harris took Phil Sherman off the case, telling the PI he'd tired of throwing good money after bad. Sherman had the gall to ask Harris if he was feeling okay when he'd called. *Like he thought I was sick or something!*

Harris took up watching Seba and Vaii himself.

On Tuesday it was late afternoon before Vaii picked Seba up at the Physics building. Harris followed them to one of the dining halls.

Then he sat and waited. And waited. He obsessively kept checking through the window for fear he'd miss them leaving through some other exit. They were leaned toward one another as if having an intense conversation, though he couldn't tell whether they were arguing or professing their love for one another.

No kissing though.

In either case, the girl's relationship with Seba promised to provide a lever Harris could use to moderate the young man's attitude.

He rose and peeked in the window again. They were getting up. He watched until he could be sure they were coming out the same door they'd entered, then moved ahead along the path he thought they'd follow toward Seba's dorm. He called up a satellite view of the area on his phone, then contacted his SUV and had it move to a spot close to their presumed course.

A spot he thought would be relatively secluded.

~~~

"...and when companies call, you've been telling them we'll build test engines for them?!" Arya asked, surprised.

Kaem nodded, "Small ones."

"I thought we weren't going to give them any other samples until they agreed to pay for the patent?"

Kaem shrugged, "I think they're having a really hard time coming to grips with the material properties. After all, it'd be a disaster for them to agree to pay a fortune, then find out that the only shape we can make's a flat 1mm thick plate." He snorted, "I think they fear being like the proverbial farmer that paid good money for a 'surefire' organic way to kill crop insects—which subsequently turned out to be instructions to put a bug on one stone and squash it with another. They want to be absolutely sure we can build a workable engine out of stade." He glanced at her, "Did we get our trademark on 'Stade' yet?"

Arya gave a dismissive wave as if it weren't important, "Yeah, now you can put a 'TM' symbol on it anytime you use it." She gave him a concerned look, "But, how do you think we're going to afford these test engines?"

"Oh. I told them they had to make the glass molds for the engines. Gunnar can silver the glass and I told them we can 'pour' stade into the molds."

Arya frowned, "Pour?!"

"I told them that wasn't exactly how it worked, but if they make us molds that we'd be able to pour full of material, that they'd work for our method."

"Can we afford that much silver?"

"Mirrors don't use that much silver. Besides, I told them they'd have to call you and you'd make them prepay."

Laurence E Dahners

"How much?"

"Current price of gold by volume. Believe me, we'll come out *way* ahead. At the price of gold by volume, the test samples we sent them would cost over $10,000 each. If several companies decide they want test engines before committing themselves, we'll be able to afford a patent by ourselves."

"You think they'll pay that much?"

Kaem shrugged, "They will if they've got any sense. Besides, the price will make them want to do their tests using smaller motors. Engines small enough Gunnar can silver them without building another entire setup."

"How do we get the glass back out of them?"

"That's *their* problem. I pointed out they could either break or melt the—" Kaem stopped talking when someone stepped out on the path in front of them.

Harris! Arya thought. *What's he want now?*

Hair standing up in clumps, Harris looked raggedy and wild-eyed. He said, "I'd like to have a confidential conversation with you two." He nodded to one side where a vehicle stood with its doors open, "If you'll get in my SUV, we'll just go have a nice talk."

Kaem moved to the other side of the sidewalk, and sped up, saying, "Sorry, Mr. Harris, we're just not interested."

Harris stepped closer saying, "I have a gun." He pulled a pistol partly out of his jacket pocket then shoved it back in. He waved his other hand toward the SUV. "No need to get excited. I only want to talk."

"Shit!" Kaem said resignedly, eyes on Harris's jacket pocket.

Arya considered their situation. She knew several techniques for disarming an assailant but they were risky and none of them applied to a gun that was inside a jacket pocket where she couldn't get a grip on it. On the other hand, she'd been repeatedly told not to go to a, presumably secluded, location with a kidnapper. That forfeited the help of bystanders. And, she thought Harris looked like he'd lost touch with reality. She said, "We're not going anywhere with you."

Harris had Kaem by the arm and was pushing him toward the SUV. To Arya, he said, "I don't really give a damn whether *you* come or not. But, if you don't come, I'll have to kill you so you can't raise an alarm."

Arya saw Kaem shoot her a frightened/questioning glance, as if he thought she'd know what to do. *Why didn't I consider the possibility of a gun? Americans love weapons!* Then Kaem was getting in the passenger seat of the SUV. Harris was waving impatiently for her to approach. His gun hand was still in the pocket, but she could see the barrel of the pistol tenting the material.

As best she could tell it was pointed right at her.

And a crazed man had his finger on the trigger.

She said, "Well this isn't like a Hawaiian vacation."

Kaem and Harris both gave her confused looks.

~~~

Sylvia said, "911 operator. What's your emergency?"

No one answered, but when Sylvia listened carefully, she could hear a man in the background giving orders. "Open the door and get in!"

A female resignedly spoke from closer to the phone. She said, "Yes, sir."

Sylvia heard what sounded like a car door open, then she heard a second door open. The first voice said, "Stay in your seats while I get in." A moment later Sylvia heard two car doors close and the timbre of the sounds she was hearing changed. *Whoever's calling just got in a car. And it sounds like she was* told *to get in.* Sylvia pressed the button to call her supervisor.

As Sylvia listened, the man gave an address to the car's AI. Sylvia wrote it down.

Her supervisor arrived at her side, "What's going on?"

Sylvia told her AI to copy the call to her supervisor's headset. "I think this is a code-phrase call, made by a phone's AI. When the call connected, the caller didn't report an emergency but I heard a man's voice directing a woman to get in a car." She showed the supervisor the address she'd written down. "The man told the car to drive to this location. I'd like to scramble an unmarked car to that location to wait for them to arrive. And a car to try to follow them there: the phone's sending us GPS location data."

Her supervisor nodded, "Send some backup too. It's dark, so even marked cars would be hard to recognize as police if they keep their flashers off."

~~~

Harris had the kid and his girlfriend get in the front seats of his SUV. He got in behind them so he could keep them covered with his gun. A quick conversation with his AI started the vehicle toward an address near a hunting cabin he'd stayed in before.

Once they were underway, he said, "I hope you guys'll relax. I *just* want to talk. Sorry to have to do it this way, but," he tried to control his temper but knew his exasperation showing in the tone of his voice, "you shot down *all* my earlier efforts... Acted like assholes too."

The girl's eyes were narrowed and she looked concerned.

The kid said, "What do you want to talk about?"

"I'm *offering* to help you develop your new material for the market. You're trying to do it by yourselves, right?"

"Yes," the kid said dismissively. "We *don't* need help."

"You have no business experience. I'm sure you don't have sufficient funding since I find you on a list of Curtis scholars. It's common knowledge those are only awarded to financially destitute students."

"Nonetheless, we're doing fine."

"*We've* realized that what you've done is induce another state of matter. That somehow you can turn water into something completely different. 'Ice,' so to speak, but incredibly hard and strong."

The kid said, "Okay, so?" He didn't sound surprised. Nor dismayed that someone knew their secret.

"Once people realize this's just a different state of matter, which after all isn't too difficult to figure out since it has exactly the same density as water, it'll only be a matter of time before they figure out how to do the same thing."

"I don't think so."

Getting more irritated, Harris said, "*Besides,* we've discovered a way to make your wonder material fail catastrophically." This time Harris saw them glance at one another as if they were finally surprised, and perhaps concerned.

Tightly the kid asked, "And what's that?"

"*That's* something I can tell you once we're on the same team. A lack of that knowledge would be a disaster for you if you sell this stuff and people start building important projects out of it. When those projects fail disastrously, you're going to be subject to astronomical lawsuits."

"Why wasn't this in your report?"

"We thought of a few more tests to undertake after you picked up your results. Since you'd left the specimens behind, we did those tests a couple of days after that. The outcomes were alarming."

For some reason, upon hearing that, rather than tensing further, Seba seemed to relax. He said, "Okay, thanks for letting us know."

Having expected more consternation, Harris pushed the issue. "This… test turned your samples back into water! I'd think you'd be more concerned about what could happen if such an event occurred with one of your products while it was being used in, say a rocket engine."

"Uh-huh," the kid said calmly. "We'll have to keep that from happening."

Harris exploded, "You don't even know what we did!"

"What'd you do?"

"I'm not going to tell you *now*! That knowledge is one of the things I'm bringing to the table! I want to negotiate a deal to help you by providing financing and business acumen in return for a piece of the company we build together. Learning what can destroy your product is simply a minor benefit I'll be providing alongside those two. I absolutely *guarantee* the value of my contribution will be far greater than my share of the income!"

~~~

Sylvia and her supervisor had been listening to this conversation between the two men with more and more confusion. "Wonder materials… new states of matter… catastrophic failures. It sounded like an argument of some kind but not an emergency. She'd have sworn she'd heard a girl's voice initially but she hadn't heard it lately. She looked up at her supervisor, "I'm going to try querying the caller again?"

Her supervisor nodded.

Sylvia pressed a button to connect her mic and said, "This is the 911 operator. *Do* you have an emergency?"

~~~

In her earbud, Arya heard what the 911 operator said but didn't think she could answer directly without tipping Harris off to what was going on. She pondered a moment...

Harris was startled when the Seba's girlfriend suddenly spoke. "Kaem, I think this's a good idea. Let's accept his offer."

Seba looked startled. "No," he began.

Before Seba could say more, the girl turned toward the back seat. Speaking pleasantly, she said "Mr. Harris, it's really difficult to talk about this while you're pointing a gun at us. Would you mind putting it away?"

Though she'd spoken as if putting the gun down was a completely reasonable thing to do, the idea made Harris fretful. He swung the gun to one side, setting it on the seat next to him but keeping his hand on it. "I'll stop pointing it at you," he said, feeling like he'd been as reasonable as he could be in return.

~~~

Sylvia looked up at her supervisor. "Gun!"

Her supervisor said, "I'll let the cars know. You try to give our victim advice."

Sylvia nodded and pressed her mic button. "Okay, it sounds like you're being kidnapped. We have police responding. Try to keep your kidnapper calm."

~~~

The girl turned and looked Harris in the eye. She said, "Thank you. That makes me feel a lot better. Can you tell us where you're taking us?"

"No," he said truculently, immediately regretting his tone after she'd sounded so easy-going.

She tilted her head curiously, "Aren't you worried that *forcing* us at gunpoint to go somewhere against our will is going to make us less likely to agree to work with you?"

"No!" he tried to calm himself. "No. Once you understand what I'm proposing, you're going to be *overwhelmed* by the deal I'm giving you!" *I'm being too emphatic,* he thought.

"Okay," she said pleasantly, "do you have a contract you can pass forward for us to read over? Something that outlines your plans for our new company and outlines your contributions?"

~~~

Sylvia pressed a button and notified the entire team following the incident that the kidnapper was "passing papers forward" suggesting he was in the backseat and his victims were in the front.

~~~

Harris gave the girl a suspicious look. He'd expected he'd have to engage in a lot more argument before he could bring them to the point of reading through the contract. She smiled back pleasantly. He forced himself to smile and said, "As a matter of fact I do." Using his left hand, he unlatched and fumbled in the briefcase he'd brought with him. Finding one of the folders with copies of the contract he'd drawn up, he passed it up to Seba. "Here. Have a look. We've got a little time before we get to where we're going. You should have enough time to get some idea of what I'm offering."

Affably, the girl asked, "Do you have a copy *I* can look at? Kaem and I are partners, so I'd need to approve it as well."

Harris reached his left hand back into the briefcase and produced another folder.

When he passed it up, she took it, thanking him. "Do you have a couple of pencils we can use to mark-up sections we're concerned about?"

He found some pencils in the briefcase and passed them up front as well.

She asked the car to turn on the seat lights so they could read.

Harris found himself nervously wanting to talk. "I'm sorry about what I've had to do to get your attention. But I just *had* to offer my services. This contract's a *really* great deal for you guys," he said. "You'd be gaining my experience and access to the network of professionals I already have business contacts with. We'd be able to help you market your material widely; then evaluate, compare, and contrast competing bids. I'd be bringing a wealth of business expertise to contract negotiations—"

"That's a good point, Mr. Harris," the girl said. "Shouldn't we have someone evaluate *this* contract for us? I mean, besides ourselves? You're pointing out, and rightly so, that you'd be the one to help us evaluate outside contracts if you joined our company, but who do we have evaluate the contract we'd be signing with you?"

Harris felt a tightness in his stomach. He tried not to growl, but knew his tension was coming through as he said, "You don't *need* to have anyone evaluate this contract. I wrote it in the best interests of both Mr. Seba and myself. If you're part of the package with Mr.

Seba, we can just add you to that side of the agreement."

~~~

Sylvia said, "Go easier on him. You shouldn't antagonize an angry man with a gun."

~~~

Though Harris worried that he'd been overly emphatic in his claims, the girl cheerfully said, "Oh, okay. Can you give us a little while to read through this?"

"Sure," Harris said. He tried to calm himself so he could wait quietly.

Despite his resolution to remain silent, a few moments later he found himself asking, "Any questions? I'll be happy to explain anything that's not clear."

"No, I just need time to read it," the girl said.

"How about you Mr. Seba?" Harris asked.

"Um, yeah," he said, "just need some time to read."

The girl had been writing on the contract with her pencil. Now she leaned toward Seba and said, "Did you notice this?" She was tapping on the contract with her pencil.

Harris leaned forward to see which paragraph she was concerned about. She was tapping on a paragraph right next to where she'd written in the margin. However, when he leaned forward, she straightened up, pulling her copy of the contract back over to her side of the vehicle.

She said, "Although, that does seem like a pretty good deal for us, don't you think?" She flipped the pencil over and started to erase what she'd written.

Suddenly suspicious, Harris leaned forward. Reaching out, he said, "Let me see that!"

"It was nothing," the girl said, continuing to erase.

Harris found his right hand bringing the gun around. He pointed it at the girl. "I *said*, 'Let me see that!'"

Timidly, the girl said, "You're pointing your gun at me again? I thought we were—"

"Yes, I'm pointing my goddamned gun! And you'd better be glad that's *all* I'm doing! Give me that contract *now*!"

~~~

Sylvia said, "Stay calm. Speak placatingly. Your car's almost arrived at the address he gave it when he got in. We have the police waiting there and more arriving soon. If you can talk him into getting out of the car that would be ideal."

~~~

The girl gave Harris the contract she'd been working on and he held it up to the light. He couldn't read most of what she'd erased, but he could make out the word "psychotic." He grabbed at her hair. It was so short he didn't get a grip on his first attempt. Grabbing again and twisting for a tighter grip, he jerked her head back and leaned up close to her face. "You think I'm *crazy*?!"

Unbelievably, she said calmly, "Oh, no. You must be misreading something I wrote."

The car had been slowing. Now it said, "We've arrived at your destination."

Feeling overwhelmed, Harris found himself shouting. "You wrote *something* about 'psychotic'!"

"That's not what I wrote," she said soothingly. "If you'll give it to me I'll try to figure out what I might have written that looks like that."

In a brittle tone, Harris said, "You're even talking to me like you think I'm crazy!"

"My goodness," the girl said cheerfully, ignoring the way he'd twisted her neck, "I think we've arrived at our destination. Should we get out?"

"No!" Harris shouted. Calming himself, he said, "Climb over into the right seat with Seba. I've got to drive us a little farther on manual."

For the first time, the girl sounded upset. "You want me to sit in his *lap*?"

"Yes!" Harris said, wondering why she'd object to sitting in her boyfriend's lap.

"I can drive a car on manual," she said grimly. Then, sounding calm again, "Wouldn't that be better for you? You could stay in the back seat and cover us with your gun. Keep us from doing anything foolish." She turned forward and took the wheel, "Just tell me where you want to go."

Harris felt like she was tricking him, but more distressingly he felt like he was losing control of the situation. There was too much going on! He took a deep breath. *It* would *be a lot easier if she drove,* he thought. But, before they drove the rest of the way to the hunting cabin, he knew he needed to disengage the AI and tell it to stop recording their location. Abruptly, he said, "Okay. You'll drive... Car AI."

The feminine voice of the car's AI said, "Yes? How may I help?"

"Disengage yourself to allow manual driving."

"Disengaged," the AI said.

"Shut yourself down and stop recording our GPS location."

The AI said, "I'm unable to do that."

"Goddammit!" Harris said, seething with frustration. He knew there were commands that would do what he wanted. Hell, people *insisted* on the availability of manual driving without GPS recording so they could have affairs. But the damned car's AI wasn't smart enough to take commands that didn't fit its menu of choices. He tried again, "Disconnect AI and GPS."

Again, the damned AI said, "I'm unable to do that."

Frustrated, Harris punched the seat in front of him. Suddenly, the girl said, "AI, stop recording GPS."

The AI said, "GPS recording discontinued."

The girl said, "AI shut down."

"Shutting down," the AI said.

Feeling quite discombobulated by her cooperation in spite of the fact she thought he was crazy, Harris said, "Thanks. Now drive on down to the next crossing road and turn right.

~~~

Sylvia tried to sound soothing, "It's okay. Our guys will follow. He's probably going to get you out of the vehicle. If and when that happens, and if you can do it without getting him excited, put some distance between yourself and your captor."

Arya felt a shiver run over her as she realized the 911 operator was asking her to give the police a shot at Harris.

~~~

Officer Melnick and his rookie partner Rose had watched the SUV pull up and stop near the mailbox for the old farmhouse across the road. The lights were on in both front seats, revealing the two people there. They weren't lit brightly enough to tell much, but Melnick had the impression they were young. From what Sylvia had told them, the perp had been passing papers forward, presumably to the two people up front. The shadowy figure in the second row of seats had to be the kidnapper.

Laurence E Dahners

No one got out. Melnick had his AI connect him to Sylvia at emergency dispatch. "What's going on?"

"He's having the girl drive the car somewhere on manual with GPS recording disconnected."

"Crap!" Melnick said. There were probably some legitimate reasons to do such a thing, but he couldn't imagine any *innocent* reasons for doing it in this situation. "Do you have any idea how far? I'm trying to figure whether we should get out and follow on foot or should we follow in the car?"

"No idea Joe, sorry."

Melnick spoke to the police car's AI and, after making sure it would leave all lights off, told it to follow the other car at a distance of 200 feet. That was about as far back as it could reliably distance check another vehicle with its bumper radar.

~~~

As she eased the SUV back onto the road, Arya wondered whether she could wreck it somehow, thus bringing it to a stop. After all, even though she had quite a bit of experience with manual driving, most people didn't. It wouldn't be too remarkable if someone wrecked a car doing it. But the frenetic way Harris had been acting made her reluctant to do anything that might set him off.

She glanced up into the rearview mirror, wondering whether the police that the 911 operator said were waiting at that address were following or not. She didn't see any lights. *If they're following on foot, I hope Harris isn't going to make me drive very far.*

~~~

Harris rubbed at his temple, feeling like his head was about to explode. "Why're you going so slow?" he asked suspiciously.

"I'm pretty sure it's safer," the girl said. "Driving on manual's supposed to be dangerous, right?"

Harris desperately wanted to get off the road and down to the hunting cabin. *Nobody knows where we are,* he reminded himself. Then he made a counterargument with himself. *But once we get to the cabin, nobody'll even be able to find us.* Trying to distract himself, he asked Seba, "What'd you think of the contract?"

The damned girl answered, "I don't think I should be trying to read it while I'm driving, should I?"

"No! No. I wasn't asking *you*. I was asking Mr. Seba what *he* thought of the contract. What about it, Mr. Seba; do you understand the benefits?"

For long moments Seba said nothing. Harris was afraid he wasn't going to answer, but then the girl gave him a nod and he spoke. "I don't really understand it very well. Maybe you could give Arya some time to explain it to me?"

What?! Is he dense?! Harris wondered. *How in the world could someone that stupid have invented that stuff?!* He took a deep breath and let it out. "We're almost there. You can have her explain it to your heart's content once we're in the cabin." Despite his attempt to speak calmly, he knew he still sounded brittle and irritated. "Slow down. Turn in on that dirt road on your left."

"Is it very far?" the girl asked as she turned the vehicle. "I've got to go to the bathroom."

Oh my God! Harris thought. *Will this petty crap never end?!* "It's only a few hundred yards! You'll just have to hold it."

~~~

Sylvia was zooming in on the map of the area. The dirt road she thought the SUV had turned off onto—basing it on the directions the perp was giving since they'd turned the GPS off—entered a large wooded piece of private property. She wasn't confident that the dirt road was properly drawn on her mapping software, but there was only one building on the property—something that looked like a small cabin.

She pressed her "all hands" button and apprised her team of the situation.

~~~

At first, Arya drove nearly as fast on the bumpy dirt road as she'd been going on the pavement. Her thought was that a hard shaking was to her and Kaem's advantage. Then she considered the fact that she had a crazed man sitting behind her with his finger on the trigger. She slowed, saying, "I guess I've been going too fast. Sorry. Just not used to this manual driving."

The rough dirt road came out of the trees and pulled up to a small cabin. Arya braked to a stop and, speaking as if she felt frantic, said, "I've gotta go! Gotta go! Can I get out? Is the cabin locked?"

Harris barked, "Wait just a *damned* minute! I'm getting out first."

Arya glanced down with just her eyes, looking for the rocker switch that would lock all the doors. Placing her finger on it she hoped against hope that Harris would close his door before opening hers so she could lock him out.

Her wish was denied. With his door still wide open, he jerked hers open as well, "Get out," he said roughly. Then he barked, "Not you, Seba, you stay in the car!"

Arya got out, moving slowly. Now she regretted rushing down the dirt road, realizing it might've left the police behind, especially if, as she expected, they were trying to follow the dirt lane with their lights out in dim moonlight. Realizing that the police vehicle's tires might make popping noises going over rocks on the dirt road, she started loudly begging in hopes of covering any sounds. "Hurry, please! I don't want to pee my pants. I've gotta go! I've gotta go." At the same time, she started rapidly shuffling away toward the cabin.

Harris lunged after her. His right hand encumbered by the gun, he used his free left hand to grab the back of her right elbow and jerk her back, saying, "Shut up! Get a ho—!"

Surprised to be jerked back, Arya made a split-second decision to use the motion Harris had initiated to attack the man.

The hard pull on her elbow started her body rotating. She lowered her center of gravity and increased the speed of the turn to make it a whirl.

She swayed further to his left, avoiding the gun in his right hand.

Then, still pivoting, she exploded up and out, driving a palm-strike into the middle of his face. She felt his nasal bones crunch as the blow cut him off mid-word.

His gun went off.

He staggered back.

As Harris fell, the gun flailed toward her—Arya thought the motion was unintentional. She swore at herself, *I should've moved with him to stay inside the swing of that weapon!*

She started to dodge.

The gun went off again.

Arya felt a hard *smack* against her chest.

The driver's window on the SUV shattered.

She dropped to the ground, wondering if he was still fighting or had simply fired the gun in reaction to getting hit in the face. *Do I play possum? Or can I attack? she wondered as she waited for the pain of the bullet that had hit her chest.*

~~~

Kaem had been watching from the passenger seat. It'd looked like Harris was going to leave Kaem in the SUV while he walked Arya in to the bathroom. Kaem was dithering about whether he should get out and run into the woods. Or stay to try to help Arya. Hating the weakness that made him useless in a fight, he thought, *Get free yourself,* then *see if you can help Arya.*

Thus, when he saw Arya move ahead, then whirl back toward Harris, his hand was already on the door, waiting to open it and try to hustle out into the trees.

A gun went off.

The driver's-side window burst in toward him.

Shit! Kaem thought, throwing the door open and rolling out into the night. His last glimpse of Arya had shown her falling to the ground. On hands and knees, he scrambled around the front of the SUV and peeked under the bumper toward Arya.

She lay still!

Harris lay sprawled supine just beyond her.

Keeping a wary eye on Harris, Kaem scrambled crab-wise over to Arya. As he did so, he saw men running up from the road with their extended hands locked together in front of them.

Guns! Kaem thought.

One of the approaching men shouted, "Police! Down on your stomachs!"

Kaem was kneeling next to Arya. She was pressing a hand to her chest! "Are you okay?" Kaem asked apprehensively.

Arya looked up into his eyes, "I think so." She lifted her hand away from her chest and lifted her head to look down at the area. Kaem saw a hole in her coat!

"You got shot!" he said, panic-stricken.

"Yeah," she said, "but this is my 'warm' coat."

One of the policemen was screaming at him to lie flat. As Kaem slowly lowered his body, he asked, "It hit a stade and bounced off?"

She nodded, "Then it hit the window. You're not hurt, are you?"

Kaem shook his head, saying, "No. Not unless *shitting* my pants counts as an injury." He rolled his eyes at himself, thinking, *She does* not *think your jokes are funny!* Aloud, he said, "Sorry. Trying to make light of the situation and not doing it well."

A policeman knelt with a knee in the small of Kaem's back and started patting him down.

~~~

Melnick and Rose had parked their unmarked car. They were trotting up the dirt lane toward the SUV holding the presumed kidnapper and his victims when they heard a couple of gunshots. Drawing their weapons, they chambered rounds and started moving as fast as they could considering the dim lighting from a low-in-the-sky quarter moon.

Approaching with weapons at the ready, Melnick saw three people.

Closest was what looked like a man who was rolling from supine to prone and trying to push up on one hand. The other hand was clasped to his face.

A feminine form lay on her side. Someone else was on hands and knees next to her.

"Get down on your stomachs!" Melnick bellowed, pulling out his tactical flashlight with his left hand. He played the light over the scene. The man who'd just rolled over had blood dripping through the fingers clasped to his face. *That guy got shot,* Melnick thought.

Melnick's unconscious bias dismissed the girl as a possible shooter. He moved on to check out the man on his hands and knees next to her. Arriving at the man's side, Melnick screamed at him to lie flat. The guy slowly lowered himself to his stomach, still talking to the girl, though Harris couldn't really understand what he was saying. With his partner standing beside him, weapon trained on the guy's back, Melnick knelt and quickly checked him for a weapon. "Clear," he said to let Rose know it was safe. He waved, "See if the guy who got shot needs help," he told Rose. Pushing down on the man he'd just checked over, Melnick commanded, "Stay flat! Hands behind your back!"

Grabbing one of the man's hands and reaching for his cuffs, Melnick turned to the woman. *She's good-looking*, he thought with some surprise. "You okay?"

She nodded.

"You're the one who called 911?"

She nodded again.

Melnick indicated the prone guy he'd just cleared of weapons, "This is your kidnapper?"

She shook her head and used her chin to indicate the guy who'd been shot in the face.

As he turned to look that direction, Melnick was wondering, *What? Did the guy try to commit suicide?*

Oh shit! Melnick thought as he stood.

The guy with the bloodied face had a gun trained on Rose's head. Glancing at Melnick, the man said, "Drop your weapon."

Heart sinking, Melnick crouched and placed his gun on the ground. As he stood back up, he distantly noticed his hands were trembling. It was hard to read Rose's face but Melnick could tell his new partner was terrified.

The man said, "Take off your vests."

Shit, shit, shit! Melnick thought. He started slowly removing his bulletproof vest. Trying to keep his voice steady and reasonable, Melnick said, "There're a lot more police on the way, you should give yourself up before somebody gets killed and you wind up with a murder rap." Melnick winced, noticing the crazed look in the man's eyes for the first time. *I probably shouldn't have said that*, he thought. Further study revealed the man's copious bleeding all seemed to be pouring out of his nose.

It didn't look anything like a gunshot wound.

"Shut up!" the man said. "How the hell'd you bastards get here so fast?!"

Melnick hesitated. The man had, after all, just *told* him to shut up. Also, he didn't want to sell the girl down the river for calling them.

The man began, "I *said*—"

The girl stepped forward, interrupting by saying, "I called 911."

"You *bitch*...!" He paused, "Wait. How? I didn't hear you make any calls!"

She shrugged. Stepping closer to him, she said, "I have a code phrase for my phone's AI. If it hears the phrase it connects itself to 911."

Turning the weapon on her, the man stepped closer. His voice had a frenetic tone as he said, "Why would you *do* that?! Are you *insane*? I *told* you I just wanted to talk!"

Melnick slowly lowered his hand to the pepper spray on his belt and surreptitiously unsnapped its cover. To his dismay, the girl kept moving closer and closer to the man with the gun! *Step away!* Melnick thought.

As she drifted even closer the girl shrugged again, "It seemed like you were kidnapping us."

Melnick glanced at Rose who seemed paralyzed. The perp seemed totally focused on the girl so Melnick slid the pepper spray canister out of its holder on his belt, trying to keep it palmed while trying to adjust its spray to maximum distance by feel.

My God! Melnick thought as he realized the girl was only a couple of feet from the perp. The gun was centered on her chest. *Is she crazy?!* Even in the dim light, he could tell when she looked out past the perp's shoulder, saying, "Oh, shit!"

The perp started to look back over his shoulder.

Melnick was taken in too. His eyes turned in the same direction.

As soon as the perp's eyes left her, the girl lunged forward, pivoting, extending, and punching up into his temple. Distantly, Melnick observed that the evolution of her movement was quite graceful.

The gun went off. It must have missed the girl to hit something hard because Melnick heard a ricochet "whing" off into the night.

The guy was down, the girl on top of him.

The girl tossed something away.

As Melnick strode toward them he recognized that she'd cast aside the perp's gun.

She rolled the guy on his stomach. As Melnick knelt beside her she pulled the perp's wrists back and presented them.

As Melnick applied his handcuffs to the guy's wrists, he thought to himself, *This girl just saved my ass... In more ways than one,* he thought considering the fact that he'd tried to arrest the wrong person, that he and Rose had let the perp get the drop on them, and that the perp had the crazy look of the kind of guy who might've killed them. He looked her in the eye. "Thanks," he said, expressing all the gratitude he felt in that one word. Then he caught himself, "But those were some crazy risks you took, getting so close. You're really lucky he missed." He caught himself again, "He did miss, right? You're okay?"

She nodded, "I'm fine."

Sylvia was shouting in Melnick's earbud. "Melnick! What the hell's going on! We heard gunshots! We've scrambled an ambulance. Do you need it?!"

"We're okay," Melnick told her. He rolled the perp up. *Out cold!* He thought with a little surprise. *The punch the girl threw was not only elegant but it packed a wallop.* He amplified his earlier statement to Sylvia, "We need the ambulance though, for the perp. He's, uh, suffered some head trauma."

With even more respect, Melnick turned his eyes back to the girl. "Where'd you learn to fight?"

"Karate," she said.

Huh, Melnick thought. He checked the perp again. *Unconscious but breathing. This time he's properly restrained.* Melnick looked up at Rose who was staring wide-eyed. "Rose..." Melnick abruptly noticed Rose's empty holster, "Retrieve your weapon, then guard our prisoner. We don't want him lying on his cuffed wrists, so undo them and re-cuff them in front so he can lay on his back."

Melnick looked up and saw a train of headlights bumping down the dirt lane toward then. He looked back at the second man who was still lying flat on his stomach. *Compliant guy*, Melnick thought. He looked at the girl, then pointed at the man on his stomach. "That guy's okay? We can let him up?"

She nodded.

After uncuffing the other guy and telling him he could get up, Melnick turned to the girl and waved at the guy Rose was guarding, "You know who our perp is?"

"James Harris. Owner of Harris Laboratories."

Eyeing the perp, Melnick frowned as he thought about something Sylvia had said to them. "He was trying... trying to get you to sign some kind of contract?"

She nodded.

"And he thought such a contract would be enforceable?"

"I, um, think he's had some kind of... nervous breakdown. He wasn't really making much sense... He seemed really manic."

Melnick turned his flashlight slowly around the scene, noticing the shattered glass in the driver's window of the SUV. He turned back to the girl. The other guy'd come up beside her. "You two are really okay?"

She nodded, "Just a little shaken up."

The guy nodded in agreement.

"Okay," Melnick said. He raised an eyebrow, "I'd advise you *not* to punch people holding guns in the future, okay? If the shot he got off had hit you, you could be dead."

"I hope there's no more being held at gunpoint *in* my future," the girl said.

Melnick nodded affirmatively, "Me too."

~~~

Other officers were detailed to take Harris to the hospital. Melnick and Rose took the girl, Vaii, and the guy, Seba, down to the station to get their statements. According to them, Seba had invented some kind of new technology that Harris wanted a piece of. They didn't want to talk much about the technology because it was confidential, but it apparently had something to do with rocket engines.

It wasn't until they were getting ready to leave the station that the girl put her coat back on and Melnick saw the holes in it. Four holes over the left side of her chest. "Wait a minute. What happened here?" he asked, pointing at the round perforations in the cloth of the jacket.

"Nothing important," the girl said. "Just some rips in the fabric."

Melnick frowned, "Those look like bullet holes!" He held out his hand, "Let me check your coat."

Her face closed in, "I'd rather you didn't. As you can see, I'm not injured."

"Let me see your jacket. I need to understand what's going on."

"You've seen my blouse underneath. There's no blood. Even if they're bullet holes, they must be shallow, in-and-out perforations."

"Let me see the jacket," Melnick said impatiently.

"Why? Are *we* on trial now?" the girl asked.

Melnick rolled his eyes. "No, but if those are bullet holes it significantly affects the charges we'll be bringing against Mr. Harris."

"I thought kidnapping was already a bad thing to be charged with. Surely, whether or not a bullet punched a hole in the cloth of my jacket but didn't injure me doesn't affect the severity of his charges, does it?"

Melnick glanced at Seba who'd remained quiet through the entire interview except when personally put on the spot. He wasn't reacting to this either, merely watching Ms. Vaii. Melnick looked back at Vaii and he sighed, "If I were to let you get out of here with unrecorded bullet holes in your jacket the Lieutenant would have my ass."

Vaii sighed in return. She unzipped the jacket and folded it back so he could see the inside of the front left panel. Displaying, she said, "See, those holes don't go all the way through."

Saying, "Let me see," Melnick stepped close and took the folded-back panel from her, putting his finger in one of the holes on the outside and then sliding a finger from his left hand to the same location on the inside to feel for a defect. "Wait a minute," he said, raising his eyes to hers as he felt hard segments in the jacket. The finger that was lifting them told him they were too light to be metal, but... "What's this?"

"What's what?" she asked innocently.

Melnick tried to bend the segment between his fingers, expecting it to be merely firm. Instead, as he put substantial pressure on it, he realized it was completely rigid. "What the hell?"

She sighed again, "It's confidential. Can we talk about it somewhere besides your main hallway?"

~~~

Back in an interview and interrogation room, Arya said, "I sewed 3" x 6" plates of our new rocket engine material in between the inner and outer shells of my jacket. It's a great insulator, so even this lightweight jacket is nice and warm on a really cold day like today."

"And it stops bullets?" Melnick said dubiously.

"If it's strong enough to tolerate the heat and pressure inside a rocket engine, it should be strong enough to stop bullets, don't you think?" she asked reasonably.

Melnick looked at Seba but he returned an expressionless look. Melnick reached a hand out to Arya and said, "Take off the jacket so I can examine it, please."

"No."

Irritated, Melnick said, "Let me see it!"

"What are you charging me with?" she asked.

"I'm not charging you with anything," Melnick said, getting more frustrated. "I just... need to examine the *evidence*."

"Evidence of what?" she asked.

"That you were shot!"

"As I've told you, I *wasn't* shot. The materials in this jacket are confidential. I don't intend to let you examine them, nor to let you keep them. I will be perfectly satisfied if Mr. Harris is administered justice appropriate to kidnapping and any charges of shooting at or near me are dropped."

"I've got to impound that jacket as evidence!"

"I demand my right to legal counsel."

"You don't stand accused of any crimes!"

"Yet you're intending to deprive me of my property. I believe I have a right to an advocate in this situation."

Having never confronted such circumstances, Melnick felt uncertain. "Let me go talk to my Sergeant. I'll be right back."

As soon Melnick left the room, Kaem said, "Let me have the jacket."

"Why?" Arya asked, nonetheless taking off the jacket.

Kaem flipped the jacket inside out. Using his pocket knife, he deftly slit and stripped out its liner in two big pieces. Within a minute he'd pulled out Arya's vest of stade plates. Kaem quickly pulled off his shirt and slipped on the stade vest. He pulled his shirt back on over the vest, then picked up the segments of the liner from Arya's jacket and stuffed one into each of the jacket's pockets. He handed her the jacket. As he slipped his own coat back on, Kaem said, "When the officer returns, tell him you changed your mind and you'll let him keep the jacket for evidence. Try to put it in the evidence bag yourself."

Wide-eyed, she said, "That's never going to work! You've seen how he wants to feel the plates himself!"

Kaem shrugged, "The worst that can…" He broke off as the door to the room opened.

Melnick stepped inside, but as he opened his mouth, Arya said, "I've changed my mind. You can keep the jacket for evidence."

Melnick gave her a surprised look, but then said, "Great, I'll just get a bag." He stepped out of the room and returned a few seconds later with a large bag, a stapler, and some labeling tape.

Arya bundled up the jacket and when Melnick held the bag open she stuffed it in. "May we go now?"

"Would you like a ride—"

"No," she interrupted. "We'll call an Uber."

Melnick let them out of the room and walked them to the front door of the police station. She had her phone call the Uber while they were walking.

"Thank you for letting us keep the jacket," Melnick said. "Pieces of evidence like that can be tremendously important at trial."

Arya rolled her eyes, "Don't try to butter me up. I like that jacket and I'm still not happy."

Outside it was cold. Once they'd gone about 10 feet, Kaem took off his jacket and handed it to her. "Oh," she said, "after destroying my jacket, the gentleman lets me borrow his."

"You weren't going to get to keep it. At least I saved the stades." He cocked his head as if noting the sensation, "Wow, they really do keep you warm."

"I told you so," Arya said. "Wait, how do you know I wouldn't be able to keep my jacket?"

"My dad told me to read up on the law as it applied to getting arrested. As you may know, young black men get arrested a lot. His theory is that things go a lot better if you know your rights and don't act like an asshole, demanding rights you don't actually have."

"So, you're saying the police can keep our property?"

"As evidence in a case, yeah."

"Don't they have to pay us for it?!"

"No. In some states they're supposed to return it to you after court." He shrugged, "Virginia's not one of those... Hey," he gave her a close look, "even if the stades kept them from penetrating, didn't it hurt getting hit by those bullets?"

She barked a laugh, "Oh, hell yes. I think the second one hit close to an edge, tilting the stade it hit. I'm pretty sure I'm gonna have a hell of a bruise in the morning."

~~~

Back in the station, Melnick pulled the jacket out of the bag, dying of curiosity about the plates in the bag. His suspicions began when he started to unroll it and it didn't seem lumpy any more.

A few minutes later he was shaking his head as he stared at the liner-less jacket and the two rags of liner he'd pulled out of the pockets. *Son of a bitch,* he thought. For a few moments he wondered whether he should try to track them down and demand the plates.

Then he shrugged and put the jacket back in the bag. *I guess not. They aren't the criminals and this's the part of the jacket that has the bullet holes.*

Epilogue

They were almost to Kaem's dorm when Arya turned to him. She looked a little dazed. "My phone took a message while Harris was pointing that gun at me."

Kaem's heart sank. "What now?"

"Space-Gen wants us to build them some engines, starting with a test version."

"Oh, okay."

"They also want to pay us a million dollars just to have a 'right of first offer' to buy rocket engines once we prove we can build them."

Holy shit! Kaem thought, but he schooled his face to stillness. "Tell them a million will hold those rights for a week."

"Really?!"

Kaem nodded. "They'll jump on it," he said, trying to sound confident.

"Okay, I'll call them Monday."

"Call them now. They're in the Pacific time zone and they called us when it was evening here. They'll still be waiting." *I hope...* Kaem thought.

As they walked into Kaem's dorm, Arya had her phone return the call. She paced back and forth in the lobby, intermittently talking to someone in California.

Kaem sat, hoping he looked calm. He felt like his head was about to explode.

Arya turned to him. "A million a week until they get us the mold for their test engine? Then no payments until we fill it with Stade and they can start testing?"

Kaem nodded. "Make the deal."

A few minutes later Arya sprawled into the big chair next to him. Looking stunned, she said, "They're sending a contract!"

Kaem took a moment to savor the news. "We should show it to an attorney."

"It's the weekend. There's no attorney to show it to. What we *should* do, is go have a drink to celebrate."

"Um…" Kaem hesitated, "I don't like alcohol."

"We'll just wet your lips with a toast of celebratory champagne. I'll call Gunnar as we walk."

I didn't say I'd go! Kaem thought, as Arya pulled him to his feet and dragged him after her.

"He says he'll meet us there!" Arya said enthusiastically.

They walked quietly for a bit, then Arya asked, "What's gotten into you?"

"What do you mean?"

"Mr. talkative, who always makes a stupid joke, gets a bit of good news and it completely shuts him up. Do I need to hold good tidings in reserve against those times when you're being annoying?"

Kaem sighed, "I don't know. Maybe. This whole thing with Harris… it's getting me down. Do you know if we can file for the patent without using my real name? I know you said it has to be in the name of a person, not our company, but… I'd rather I didn't have a bunch more crazy people coming after me."

"I don't think so, but I'll look into it. I think you'll have to do something like the movie stars do. Take a 'stage name' so to speak. Even though a lot of them have some exotic name they put on the marquees of theaters, they still live their legal lives by their boring original name. For you, it'd be kind of the opposite.

'Kaem Seba' would be the legal name of that famous guy who invented stade. Meanwhile you'd live your dull and obscure life as Joe Blow."

Kaem grinned, "'Dull and obscure...as Joe Blow' huh? Who's got the stupid jokes now?"

Still walking, Arya threw an arm around his shoulders and squeezed. "Just trying to cheer you up."

Electricity shot through Kaem at the contact. She'd virtually never touched him before. He desperately wanted to put an arm around her waist.

He refrained.

As they walked up to the bar Arya said, "You have any plans for the weekend?"

"No, what's up?" Kaem asked eagerly.

~~~

Cursing herself, Arya wondered, *Am I his* only *social life?* She said, "It's just that I'll be out of town this weekend and wondered whether you'd be okay? It's probably not so dangerous now that Harris's off the streets, but...?"

"I'll be fine," he said quickly. "Where are you going?"

"Can you mostly stay in? You know, to stay safe?"

"Yes..." he said slowly. Then, sounding worried, "Where're you going?"

"Um... I'm going to see my parents." *And the boy they think I should marry,* she thought, dreading it. But her parents thought they were doing what was right and in her best interests... and she loved them too much to say no.

~~~

Gunnar found them in a booth at the back of the Cavalier Buffalo. Though he had a tendency to think of them as a couple, they were sitting on either side of the table. Not wanting to offend, Gunnar slid in next to

Laurence E Dahners

Seba. He looked at Vaii, "So, you said when I got here you'd give me some good news?"

The girl launched into an enthusiastic explanation of how they were being paid $1 million per week. "That's $10,000 a week to you for your 1% Mr. Schmidt, merely to give Space-Gen a 'right of first offer' to buy the engines."

"Right of first offer?" Gunnar asked, not certain what that meant.

"It means that if Orbital Systems offers us $100 million for the right to buy stade rocket engines, we first have to give Space-Gen the opportunity to outbid them."

"Son of a bitch!" Gunnar breathed. He glanced at Seba who looked practically morose. Turning his eyes back to Vaii, Gunnar waved at Seba and said, "What's gotten into him?"

Vaii laughed. "Nothing like a bit of good news to put the man in the dumps!"

Gunnar turned to Seba, "Really?"

Seba shrugged, "We had a little run-in with Harris this evening. Made me think there might be some downsides to being rich and famous."

Gunnar snorted. "There'll probably be some upsides too, you know?"

Seba shrugged.

Gunnar turned to Arya, "What're you going to do with your share of the money?"

"Build the business. I'm going to make Staze the world's biggest corporation."

"I thought you were going to sell it to Space-Gen?"

"We're only selling them rocket engines and cryogen tanks. They won't be able to make them for themselves.

Anyone else wants something made of stade, they're going to have to come to us too."

Gunnar turned to Kaem, "What about you? What're you going to do with that money?"

This brought a small smile to his lips. "First thing on my list is gene therapy. Assuming I survive that... *then* I'd like to build stuff out of stade."

Gunnar was about to ask about the "gene therapy" wish when the waitress settled a tray before them. It had a bottle and some wine glasses on it. She said, "Sorry we don't have any champagne flutes." She shrugged, "Well, we don't actually have any champagne either, just sparkling wine. Is that okay?"

"It'll be fine," Vaii said. "When you pop the cork, be sure to spray some of the foam on the sourpuss in the corner, okay? There'll be a substantial tip in it for you."

"Really?" the waitress asked, studying Kaem as if she wanted to be sure he wouldn't object but he didn't seem to notice.

"Really," Vaii said.

The girl set to work on the cork. When it popped it hit the wall over Kaem and dropped in his lap. It startled him, but was nothing to the spray of bubbly foam that followed. Startled, he drew back in horror, but then, realizing what was going on, he finally broke into a huge smile.

Laughing, Vaii said, "Thanks!" and held a $100 bill out to the waitress.

As the girl walked away, Arya leaned forward and confidentially said, "I used to work as a waitress and always promised myself that when I got some money, I'd leave a big tip." She looked after the departing waitress. "Someday I'm gonna leave a lot bigger tip than that."

Laurence E Dahners

Gunnar laughed, "You haven't got money yet!"
~~~

Remembering his father's advice, Kaem kept the smile on his face. After a bit he started to feel better. *How can I be sad?* he wondered. *It looks like Stade's going to be everything I hoped for!*

The End

Hope you liked the book!

Try the next in the series, The Thunder of Engines (A Stasis Story #2)

To find other books by the author try Laury.Dahners.com/stories.html

Author's Afterword

This is a comment on the "science" in this science fiction novel. I've always been partial to science fiction that poses a "what if" question. Not everything in the story has to be scientifically plausible, but you suspend your disbelief regarding one or two things that aren't thought to be possible. Essentially you ask, "what if" something (such as faster than light travel) were possible, how might that change our world?

I think the rest of the science in a science fiction story should be as real as possible.

Therefore, in this story, the central question continues to be what if someone invented a way to stop time in a certain volume of space-time.

Stasis is not a new idea in science fiction. Niven's "slavers" used it to escape from bad situations into the future. In Vernor Vinge's *The Peace War,* people who threaten the authoritarian government are "bobbled" in stasis fields to get them out of the way. In both of these SF universes, the stasis fields are indestructible but—to the best of my recollection—they are only used to protect oneself from destruction (Niven) or also to punish offenders by sending them forward in time (Vinge) and are always spherical. Sometimes a story will use stasis for the preservation of food or people but they usually ignore the presumed mechanical properties.

The question in this book then becomes: What if these indestructible segments of space-time could be induced in non-spherical shapes. Wouldn't this provide the ultimate material for rockets, construction and other engineering projects requiring exotic properties?

Acknowledgments

I would like to acknowledge the editing and advice of Gail Gilman, Nora Dahners, Juli Damazo, Philip Lawrence, Abiola Streete, and Henrie Timmers, each of whom significantly improved this story.

Laurence E Dahners

Other Books and Series

by Laurence E Dahners

Series

The Ell Donsaii series
The Vaz series
The Bonesetter series
The Blindspot series
The Proton Field series
The Hyllis family series

Single books (not in series)

The Transmuter's Daughter
Six Bits
Shy Kids Can Make Friends Too

For the most up to date information
go to
Laury.Dahners.com/stories.html

Made in the USA
Las Vegas, NV
17 August 2022

53414043R00095